D0350600

LAYOVER

LAYOVER

AMY ANDELSON & EMILY MEYER

CROWN
NEW YORK

This is a work of fiction. Names, characters, places, and incidents either are the product of the authors' imagination or are used fictitiously. Any resemblance to actual persons, living or dead, events, or locales is entirely coincidental.

 Published in the United States by Crown Books for Young Readers, an imprint of Random House Children's Books, a division of Penguin Random House LLC, New York.

Crown and the colophon are registered trademarks of Penguin Random House LLC.

Visit us on the Web! GetUnderlined.com

Educators and librarians, for a variety of teaching tools, visit us at RHTeachersLibrarians.com

Library of Congress Cataloging-in-Publication Data is available upon request.
ISBN 978-1-5247-6487-6 (trade) — ISBN 978-1-5247-6489-0 (ebook)

Printed in the United States of America
10 9 8 7 6 5 4 3 2 1
First Edition

Random House Children's Books supports the First Amendment and celebrates the right to read.

To family . . . both the ones we are born into

and the ones we create

FLYNN

It's become my favorite sound in the world—the soles of my shoes slapping the pavement erratically. It's December, which means it's freezing, and it's dusk, which means it's going to be dark soon. But the thing is, I don't care. My cheeks flush and burn against the evening air, and I don't wait for the signal to change before bounding across Seventy-Third Street. I just . . . go.

It started a few weeks ago. I don't know how it happened, but it was like something entirely out-of-body came over me. One minute I was staring at my computer screen, and the next I was tying my running shoes. And then I just took off. I ran past Rosie in the kitchen, humming while she prepared her famous Irish stew, past Poppy in the den watching *My Fair Lady* for the millionth time, and past the Warhol hanging in the foyer. I ran past Eddie at the front door, starting his five o'clock shift, hopped back and forth impatiently until the rush hour traffic slowed down . . . *come on, come on, come on* . . . and then I took off.

In my nearly sixteen years, I had never gone running. But here I am. Running. Every day at dusk. It can't be the morning or afternoon. It has to be dusk. I like seeing the last bit of daylight escape the sky. I like that I know I probably shouldn't be running alone at this hour but that I do it anyway. I like that I'm actually a terrible runner—I get out of breath, my cheeks get bright red, and I never know when to speed up or slow down. I like that the only thing I think while I'm running is *right-left-right-left-right-left.*

I don't have to think about why Ms. Barnett gave me a B-minus on my *House of Mirth* paper, or why Aisha and Sabrina are suddenly in on some private joke that doesn't pertain to me. I don't have to think about Dad and Louisa and our upcoming Christmas break trip. I need a break all right. But what I need is a break from all the madness—theirs, mine, all of it. Right now the only place I can be is no place. Transient. Free.

Of course, when it feels like my lungs are going to burst, and it's getting too dark, I come home. I may feel crazy, but I've lived in this city long enough now to know that there's real crazy out there. What no one ever seems to understand about me is how scared I am. Of everything.

I guess I hide it pretty well. I've had to ever since that rainy Tuesday two years ago. It was December, two weeks before my fourteenth birthday, and my life would never be the same. I was in orchestra, rehearsing for the Winter Showcase, when suddenly the music room door opened, and there was Headmaster Hu accompanied by two people I would later learn were plainclothes police officers. The rest of the orchestra kept playing, but I froze. Something about the way Mr. Hu found my eyes in the room, and the serious expression on his face, made me know in my bones that they were there for me. I can't be sure, but I feel like I stood up from the piano even before Ms. Holmes stopped the orchestra and called out, "Flynn Barlow." I followed Mr. Hu and the others into the hallway, where they told me what I'd already suspected. Something was very wrong. There had been an accident. And in that moment, my eyes went blind, and all I could hear was the loudest, most silent scream ringing in my ears. I just kept thinking one thing: *Please, Mom, don't leave me. Do not leave me.*

The rest is all a blur—like my life was happening in slow motion and fast-forward simultaneously. It turns out there's no how-to guide for these kinds of situations. How was I supposed to know how to say goodbye forever to my mom, my friends, my home in Northern California, where I'd spent the first thirteen years of my life—to everything I had ever known?

Dad and Louisa arranged everything: the funeral, the flowers, the movers, the plane tickets. They're good at things like that: making calls, typing on their iPhones, telling other people what to do. Louisa even knew to show up with a black dress for me that morning, knowing I wouldn't want to wear anything in my closet. Your mother's funeral isn't exactly the type of thing you are prepared for. As we rode in the limo down El Camino Real to the service, everyone remained painfully silent. The Christmas decorations in the store windows and the trees fastened festively to the car roofs felt like a personal affront. I watched Dad, with his dark hair like mine and faraway eyes, look longingly out the window at the town he used to call home. I realized that was what Woodside, the Silicon Valley suburb with its oak-filled valleys and rolling hills, was about to become for me—a place I used to call home.

The funny thing is that my dad always used to say how much he hated New York. He'd complain every time he had to travel there for work. Maybe that was why it was so hard to imagine how his life had just moved on three thousand miles away. Even though I only visited him a few times a year, Dad always kept a bedroom for me at his and Louisa's apartment. I just don't think either one of us ever thought I'd actually live in it.

Right-left-right-left-right-left.

One of the strangest things about my new New York life was my new New York family. Of course, they weren't totally new—I'd first met Amos when I was six and he was seven. I was the maid of honor and he was the best man at our parents' wedding. It was a small luncheon at the Carlyle Hotel. I was still young enough to hope that Louisa would be walking down the aisle in some Cinderella-style princess dress. Instead she wore a simple beige sheath.

At the reception, Amos spit in my coconut cake and ignored me for the rest of the evening. One year later, Poppy arrived. I had asked Santa for a baby sister every year for Christmas, so I couldn't believe my good fortune. Despite the fact that we lived across the country from each other, I felt instantly connected to Poppy, and somehow felt compelled to protect her.

Even as a baby she seemed, I don't know, kind of sad. Louisa isn't exactly the most warm and cuddly mom—I mean, she's a perfectly nice lady, but hugs aren't really her thing. That's what they pay Rosie for, with her soft skin, sturdy frame, and old-world wisdom. The only time I ever see Louisa get really excited is when she's talking about the art she'll be auctioning at Christie's. That's how she and my dad met in the first place—he was the big bidder that night. He won the Ellsworth Kelly and took Louisa out after to celebrate. Too bad they were both married at the time. If only life were as simple as that black-and-white painting.

I guess part of me thought that moving to Manhattan would mean I'd get to spend more time with my dad. But he was always negotiating his latest tech acquisition, or attending some conference, or going to an event with Louisa. Not like I really cared. I was too gutted—trapped in a fog so deep during those first few months, I don't think I would have noticed either way. I kept doing everything I always did, like getting straight A's and practicing piano. It was just that now I missed Mom every minute of every day. I missed the frittatas she'd make with zucchini and basil fresh from her garden, the smell of her hair, and how she'd sing Joni Mitchell to herself at night when she thought I was asleep.

Right-left-right-left-right-left.

The thing about losing someone is that you want the pain of losing them to go away, but the memories to stay. You want to trick yourself sometimes and think that you don't even miss them—that maybe life can go on without them. But when you realize there could be a world without this person, even though this person was everything, then you end up feeling all sorts of sad, all over again.

But then one spring day, I started to feel a little bit better. It was the strangest thing—I was sitting on my bed, struggling to get through my *Aeneid* translation for Latin, when Amos waltzed into my room and said, "Let's go." I didn't ask any questions; I just hurried up and followed him out the door. Amos and I hadn't interacted much since I'd moved in, aside from the occasional "Pass the salt" at the dinner table, and suddenly, there we were. Hanging out. Alone. We walked for a whole ten blocks before he said anything.

"They can be such assholes."

"Who?" I asked.

"Our parents," he said with a shrug. And then: "Everyone."

We spent the rest of the day together. We wandered through Central Park in silence for hours—it wasn't awkward or anything, just comfortably quiet. We ended up all the way over in the Shakespeare Garden, where Amos guided me to an odd-shaped stone bench hidden in a corner. He led me to one end and sat me down, and then proceeded to sit at the other end, some twenty feet away. I thought it was kind of weird, but then, even though he was all the way on the other side, I heard him whisper—as if his voice were in my head—"I'm happy you're here."

I smiled. It seemed like magic. Amos explained that the Whisper Bench is one of the best-kept secrets in Central Park. Because of its unique design, if you whisper on one end, the message can be heard at the other end. The secret broke the silence between us, and Amos and I spent the rest of the day discussing anything and everything. Conversation flowed freely and didn't stop . . . until recently.

I knew all the girls on the Upper East Side idolized Amos, and after that day I could see why. With his classic features and bone structure, Amos always looks as if he's just stepped out of a Ralph Lauren ad. I know that isn't something most girls typically say about their stepbrothers, but Amos isn't most stepbrothers. And it's not as if we grew up together, sharing things like parents and holidays and genetics. He's more like this strange creature I suddenly started living with.

But it's more than Amos's obvious good looks that sets him apart. Somehow he manages to exist somewhere in between bad boy and good guy, which means that no matter where you fall on the social spectrum, you're aware of Amos Abernathy. Amos is smarter than the rest of the boys his age, and he knows it. And unlike the rest of them, Amos isn't afraid to talk about how he's feeling, or at least he isn't afraid to do that with me. Sure, he can be annoyingly smug sometimes, like when he went on a social media strike to prove some point, but when you're with him, you feel like the only person in the world.

I round the corner so now I'm running along Fifth Avenue, adjacent to Central Park, recalling how from that first afternoon on, Amos and I were basically inseparable. I traded him my classical music for his classic rock, and he introduced me to the magic of vinyl. He brought me to the best ramen in the city, and I got him hooked on peanut butter Pinkberry. On Sunday afternoons, we'd get sucked into one of Poppy's movie marathons—we'd all curl up in front of the television, and whether it was a Disney movie or a Hollywood classic, it didn't matter that Dad and Louisa weren't around. All I knew was that I finally felt like I was home.

So when I returned this past August from eight weeks at camp as a junior counselor and saw that Amos's room was empty, I assumed Louisa must be remodeling. But then Poppy poked her head in, nearly scaring me half to death, and informed me that Amos had already left for orientation at Andover. I felt sick to my stomach. In the very few, very brief emails Amos had sent me while I was away all summer, he had somehow failed to mention that he had decided to transfer to boarding school in Massachusetts for his junior year. Sure, Louisa had been pushing Andover on Amos forever, telling him that it's an esteemed Abernathy tradition, that it's what boys like him do, that it's the kind of opportunity "you simply do not pass up." But Amos had never seemed even slightly interested in doing anything particularly "Abernathy."

So imagine my surprise when he was just suddenly . . . gone. And I can't help but feel like he left because of me. Because ever since that August afternoon, I've barely heard from him. It's as if everything that happened evaporated.

My heart is still pounding from my run as the elevator doors open and I step back into our apartment.

"Flynn, time to wash up! Dinner's almost on. We've got to put some meat on those bones," Rosie calls out to me. I'm heading toward the dining room when I hear footsteps in the hall. I know these footsteps—they can belong to only one person, and mean only one thing. Amos is back.

AMOS

I don't realize how much I've missed it here until the elevator doors open into the apartment, and I smell Rosie's stew simmering in the kitchen, and I hear Poppy watching TV in the den. Life here is just as I left it. They're certainly surprised to see me. "My boy! Hurry it up, and I'll set another place at the table," Rosie says when she finally releases me from her embrace. Sure, I could have called on my way in, but the look of sheer joy on Poppy's face is pretty priceless. And I guess that's not the only reason. I head to my room, and as I walk down the hall, I see the light on in Flynn's room, the door just barely cracked open. I pause to try to hear what music she's playing—the Velvet Underground. On vinyl. Interesting.

I throw my duffel down on my bed, noting the crisp new sheets and comforter. Louisa does love her projects. I study the walls, wondering if they are a slightly lighter shade of beige than before I left. Or maybe they're darker. Whatever it is, they're different. Not like I care either way. Let Louisa have her fifty shades of beige. No one loves beige more than my mother. No one.

I can't help but feel like my room has gotten smaller. Everything in it suddenly looks so sterile, so tidy. Of course, Louisa left the Brown pennant hanging above my desk (another one of her cherished Abernathy traditions), but the lacrosse trophies, the concert ticket stubs, and all the other random paraphernalia that come with adolescence have evaporated. And it seems that my record collection has found a new home across the hall.

I've been gone for four months—the longest I've ever been away from home. I could have come back for Thanksgiving, but instead I told my mom that a bunch of the guys from my hall were going to a friend's house in Vermont. She wasn't thrilled that I wasn't coming back to the city, but with winter break just a few weeks away, she acquiesced pretty quickly.

And please, it's not like Louisa was slaving away over a twenty-pound turkey and mashing potatoes herself. Thanksgiving in the Abernathy-Barlow house plays out just like the rest of Louisa's famed dinner parties—a carefully choreographed exercise in avant-garde snobbery. Louisa does her best to play the part of the perfect hostess for the awkward gathering of extended family we never see, while Flynn, Poppy, and I push the professionally prepared food around on our Hermès patterned plates. By the time it's dessert, the kids are excused, and we sneak into the kitchen, where Rosie has stored a good old-fashioned pumpkin pie from the diner around the corner, which we eat straight out of the box.

So, as thrilling as all of that sounds, I decided that this year I'd be thankful for my solitude. The Vermont story was total BS. The truth is, I stayed on campus with the international kids, scholarship students, and weirdos like me who for one reason or another didn't want to or couldn't go home. We all just let each other be—we didn't need to pretend to be each other's stand-in family. I just wasn't ready to go home yet. But I couldn't stay away forever.

3

FLYNN

I walk through the apartment, still sweaty and trying to catch my breath, and suddenly I'm nervous to be in my own home. I pass my room—where I accidentally left the lights on and Amos's record player turning—and stand in his doorway. I watch him unpack his duffel. He looks different—the way that boys can become just, like, older overnight. Amos has always had a strong jaw and a distinct nose, but now it's like the bones of his face are even more chiseled. Or maybe it's just that his hair is longer, but somehow he looks less like the boy who left, and more like a man I'm not sure I know.

"I thought you were meeting us at the airport?" I say, feigning nonchalance. He turns around and smiles.

"I don't even get a hello?"

"Hello," I say. I look down at the parquet floor; I look up at the arched doorway. I look anywhere but straight at him.

"Madigan's having people over, so I figured I'd come in

early. And this way I can just ride to JFK with you guys tomorrow. Where are we going again? Barbados?"

"A boat in Bora Bora," I say as I tentatively take a step into his room.

"And I'm assuming the parentals are already there?"

"There was some museum opening in Hong Kong, so they left last week," I reply.

"Obviously," Amos says as he throws an Andover sweatshirt at me. "Merry Christmas."

I look at the sweatshirt—I can't tell if it's a gift or laundry. "So can I go with you to Madigan's party?" I take another step.

"Sorry, Flynn. Not tonight."

I immediately take two steps back, and practically topple onto Poppy, who apparently has been standing behind me, unnoticed. She's so stealthy sometimes it's scary.

"You're going out, Amos?" she asks, already knowing the answer. "But you just got here. Can't we spend some time together? The usual?" And in this moment, I love Poppy more than anyone else on the planet. For being so irresistibly vulnerable that even Amos, despite all his attempted bravado, can't say no to her. I don't need to turn and look at him to confirm the concession, and instead get my coat, knowing that Amos's entrance at Madigan's party has been postponed, at least for a little while. Sorry, Rosie. You'll have to save the stew for another night. For now, it will be just the three of us. Thank you, Poppy.

4

POPPY

We go around the corner to the Carlyle Hotel and fall into the leather booth of our usual table in Bemelmans Bar. Mac, our waiter, who has known me since I was in diapers, and who reminds me of that each and every time I see him, happily comes over. We order "the usual"—a hot fudge sundae, no nuts, extra sauce, three cherries. Not exactly the most nutritious dinner, but it hits most of the food groups.

Amos lets me pick out his cocktail. I read the names on the drink menu like it's an adventure novel—names that sound like faraway places or long-ago times. I've got my eye on the Jamaican Firefly, maybe because of our vacation, but change my mind and decide to go with something called the Midnight Express. Amos orders me my signature drink, a Shirley Temple in a martini glass, extra cherries.

I love that Amos knows to order my Shirley Temple in a grown-up glass to match his own. He asks Flynn if she wants hers the same way, and she shoots him a look that says, *F off.* I love that she didn't actually say the f-word. Not that I haven't heard it before. I hear it all the time. From people on the street (this is New York City), from the popular girls at school, from the rated-R movies my parents don't care if I watch, from eavesdropping on Flynn's phone conversations, and, especially lately, from Mom and Dad—that is, when they're home. But there's something about the fact that my brother and sister try not to swear in front of me that makes me feel . . . I don't know . . . loved. Still, I can tell that something is off with them. Even before Amos offended Flynn by offering her a kiddie drink. Which is exactly why I knew it was so important that we do this—that we come here. Tonight.

I love absolutely everything about hotels. I steal keys and snatch stationery and matchbooks from everywhere we stay—they're the only things I collect, besides books and movie quotes. Stickers and American Girl dolls never really interested me. I've tried, believe me, to care about the things that the other girls my age do. If only to save my mom from stressing in a way she says gives her wrinkles, and Rosie from killing so much time up at my therapist's office on the corner of First and far away. But it's useless.

Susan, my therapist, once asked me what I love so much about hotels. But I mean, where else can an almost-ten-year-old spend a Friday night in a bar? Normally, it would be inappropriate, or even against the law, for a child to be in a bar. But in a hotel anything goes: a kid has almost as much freedom as an adult (just look at Eloise). So take that, Tatiana—while your mom's tucking you and all the other girls from our class into bed at your stupid sleepover party tonight, I'm tucked into a booth at the bar in the Carlyle Hotel with my older brother and sister. Not that it bothers me that I wasn't invited—I just wish that they hadn't all brought their sleepover bags to school for the teachers and everyone else to see. Mom says girls are mean at this age, but Flynn says that's a lie—girls are mean at every age.

"Wife, mistress, or daughter?" Amos asks us as he gestures to the older man in a business suit accompanied by a pretty girl in the booth next to us.

"Daughter. Definitely daughter," Flynn declares. "He's in town for business. Lives in Chicago, keeps a place in New York. She's finishing up at Columbia. English major."

Just then the older man puts his hand on the girl's knee.

"Mistress!" we all say at the same time, and laugh. We play this game wherever we go—making up stories about people we see on the street, on the subway, even the people who come in and out of our apartment. Everyone's got a story.

Mac returns with our hot fudge sundae and three silver spoons too quickly. I do *not* want to rush this. But Amos hands me a spoon and says, "Dig in," so we do. Eventually Flynn stops pretending she doesn't want any, uncrosses her arms, and joins us. I take the tiniest bites possible—trying to see how long I can make this last. Wishing that it could be forever. I take out my vintage Polaroid camera, the one Flynn and Amos got me for my last birthday, my most prized possession, and snap a photo of the bar. I want to freeze this one moment in time so I can always remember it. Because who knows how much longer we'll have together?

AMOS

I stare at the large maritime clock on the mantel in Madigan's parents' library, willing the hands to move. They don't. They haven't all night. Or at least not since I began studying them, which was about the time that I started tuning Madigan out. And that has to have been at least ten minutes ago. But I wouldn't know, because the clock's stopped.

Madigan's midway through telling me what I've missed this semester at Collegiate. I sense that he's trying to make me regret transferring to boarding school, but his egregious retelling of the fall's non-events only reminds me of one of the reasons I wanted to leave in the first place.

"I dumped that bitch," he brutishly brags in relation to a certain Spence sophomore he was dopily chasing all last year. "I haven't cracked a book for the SATs," he asserts. Both of which, I know for a fact, are wildly untrue.

I know he's bullshitting me, because the Spence sophomore in question happens to have a sister in my Spanish class at Andover. She regaled me with stories about her wild little sister, until she heard I came from Collegiate, and made me promise not to tell Madigan that while he was building houses in Costa Rica last summer, her little sister hooked up with half of Manhattan's private-school scene in the Hamptons. She dumped him via text before Labor Day. As to the second count, Madigan's mom called Louisa for the name of my SAT tutor when his score went down two hundred points after his practice test. I know Madigan's been seeing Tom the tutor for two hours Tuesdays and Thursdays ever since.

He asks me how many girls I've banged at boarding school, and I roll my eyes in response. I'm not really in the mood to get into it with him right now, so I'll let him think what he wants.

"Seriously, dude? No one?" he asks, grinning.

The fact that Madigan lost his virginity two months before I did will go down as one of his all-time proudest achievements. Not that I've ever felt particularly competitive about that kind of stuff. I guess I've always been relatively lucky when it comes to girls. I've never really had to try too hard—the irony of somehow being labeled "hard to get." I've slept with one girl in my seventeen years, but I know people assume there have been more. Unlike Madigan, I've always been pretty private about these things.

Maybe coming home was a bad idea. I've only been back a few hours, and already my brain just feels . . . crowded. That's another reason I went away. I needed space to think. To be somewhere else. You spend your whole life in this city, and you think it's normal to never see the stars. And just as I'm trying to remember why I decided on this detour to the city in the first place, she walks in.

6

FLYNN

He just looks at me blankly, and I can't tell if he's mad or indifferent that I showed up even though he told me not to come. Is it strange that I'd rather have him be mad than indifferent? Because there's nothing worse than indifference. He takes a swig of his beer, turns back to Madigan, with his stupid popped collar, who I'm sure is boring Amos to death, and proceeds to *not* talk to me for the rest of the night. Cool, Amos.

I mean, he can't actually be mad that I'm here—Madigan's a sophomore like me, after all. And for the record, this whole party is basically populated by my friends. Or people I know. So maybe I called Sabrina and Aisha after Amos left the apartment and told them about the party. But it was only a matter of time before Madigan would text Oliver, who would then text Bennett, who would then text Sabrina, since he'll do anything to spend like five minutes alone with her. And what's

Amos so mad about anyway? He's the one who left me—I mean, us, or New York, or whatever.

As predicted, Bennett and Sabrina dip out to hook up in a guest bedroom. I catch Amos clocking their exit, too, and he at least rolls his eyes sympathetically, because he knows that now I'm stranded with Aisha. She pours us some champagne. "To sweet sixteen," she says, even though my birthday isn't until the twenty-ninth. I'm not really in the mood to celebrate, but I'm also not in the mood to stand here, awkwardly not talking to Amos, so I drink the whole cup in one gulp. I feel warm and slightly claustrophobic in my cashmere sweater, but I can't take it off, since all I've got on underneath is a grimy white camisole. Sometimes I really question my life choices. And then there's Aisha, in a little dress, just like every other girl here. They all seem pretty happy—and at the right body temperature.

"I'm so into Amos's longer hair. Is he going out with anyone at Andover? I mean, of course he is, right?" Aisha asks me in a way that doesn't really sound like a question. And since I don't know the answer, I just shrug and pour myself another round. I don't really drink much—losing control isn't exactly my thing. But lately, I'm starting to think that losing control may be exactly what I need.

Before I know it, all the edges seem a little blurred, and I realize I'm dancing with Will Dixon. I've never really cared much for dancing. The way all the girls try so hard to not seem self-conscious, while desperately attempting to get everyone's attention. It's all so forced it makes me queasy. I can feel Will's breath on my neck, and smell the Captain Morgan emanating off him—even over his aggressive cologne situation. And then I remember the other reason I hate dancing: I'm terrified of boys.

I'm about to throw Will off me, when I catch Amos's eye over Will's shoulder. And maybe because of that—because I know Amos is watching—when Will tries to pull me closer, I let him.

AMOS

It's a little after midnight when I finally make my way home from Madigan's. I didn't want to walk home with Flynn, so I waited her out. That invariably meant waiting for her lame-o friend Sabrina to emerge from a back bedroom with that dud of a boyfriend, Bennett. Then all three girls paraded out together—two of them in dumb skimpy dresses, and Flynn in that old cable-knit sweater of Jack's, her thumbs sticking out of the holes she's made in the cuffs. I've always liked that sweater on her.

It then ended up taking another half hour to extricate myself from an inane debate with a bunch of douches from Dalton about which Soho House is the best. Now I'm finally outside, and even though the air is frigid, it feels amazing. Like I can breathe again. I bury my hands in my pockets and trust my feet to find their way home. Having grown up in Manhattan, I have a certain proprietary possessiveness over these streets: my deli, my corner, my bodega, my bench in the park, my table at 21. But that's bullshit, because it's not my city—or anyone else's, for that matter. That's the thing about being away and coming back. You realize that on some level, everything has gone on without you. Which is, in its own way, comforting. It's not *my* this or that, any more than it is any other city kid's.

Except, who am I kidding? I'm not just any city kid. I'm an Abernathy. Even if my father is that lowlife Abernathy. This is a fact that, despite the dissolution of her marriage to my dad, Louisa seems intent on preserving. Frankly, she reminds me of my privileged pedigree a little too often. It's kind of gross. Like she gets off on it in some way. She appreciates the association with the fabled family way too much, if you know what I mean. Don't get me wrong—I'm certainly thankful that I had a great-great-grandfather who was at the right place at the right time when it came to real estate, publishing, women, and who knows what else. And there are certain benefits to walking around with the same last name as libraries and hospital wings. But as any Vanderbilt or Rockefeller will tell you, there's a burden to bear as well.

It's funny: while I was gone, I didn't miss the city all that much. When I left, it was all so suffocating. And I'm not just talking about the sweltering late-summer heat wave. But now that I'm back, I have the frenzy of an addict who has fallen off the wagon. I want to drink in the entire island. I feel like I could walk all night—clear down to Battery Park, up to Harlem and back. All the way till the sun rises.

And isn't this how it was always supposed to be? New York

and me. Just the two of us. It hadn't even occurred to me that I'd been wandering the streets alone, until there was someone wandering them with me. When Flynn and I started hanging out, everything changed—being with her felt like listening to a new song.

I cross Fifty-Seventh Street, remembering the time last summer when she dragged me down here for Manhattanhenge. Tourist shit like that never really interested me. The sun sets on the city every day—how could this really be such an astrophysical phenomenon? But Flynn insisted that we take part. So we stood there, and looked up at the sky, and watched the sun sink as it aligned perfectly with the east-west street. If it weren't for Flynn, I'd still be sitting in my room, texting some bullshit to Madigan.

Then she turned to me. "Do you want to hear a dumb joke?"

"Uh-oh. What?"

"Why did the cow go in the spaceship?" she asked. I rolled my eyes and shrugged. "He wanted to see the moooooon!" She smiled at me wholeheartedly.

"That's the dumbest joke I've ever heard." I laughed despite myself. I don't know if it was the orange light reflecting off the glass buildings, or standing next to her, but I was enamored. I always knew Flynn was pretty, but it wasn't until that moment that I fully appreciated how beautiful she was. And once I saw it, I couldn't un-see it. From then on, it distracted me every time I was with her. I looked at her, gazing thoughtfully up at the center of the solar system, and wondered if she was thinking about her mom.

I know it sounds messed up, but as sad as I was for Flynn, I was also jealous. At least she could properly mourn the loss of her mom. I didn't know how to process my ambivalent feelings about my dad. He'd disappeared, too. But even though he may have been a deadbeat, he wasn't dead. So because I didn't know how to think about Clay, for a long time I didn't.

But what I see now is that there's no real way to sweep things under the rug. Eventually, all the dust that's under there, and all the skeletons in the closet, come out to play. One way or another, you can't run away from reality forever.

FLYNN

It's way too early, and Poppy, Amos, and I are piled in the back of a black town car on our way to JFK. Poppy's perched in between Amos and me, tap-tap-tapping her fingers against her knee, the way she sometimes does when she's nervous. I know she hates to fly, and I know I should say something to make her feel better, but I feel like crap myself—courtesy of a solid combination of drinking too much, coming home too late, and sleeping too little.

I scroll through Instagram on my phone, and pause on a picture of Sabrina, Aisha, and me. I don't know why I let Aisha post that stupid selfie from the cab ride home (#winterbreakbitches!—I mean, really?). I check to see who liked it, and hate that I'm legitimately pleased to see that we got 102 likes. There is something seriously wrong with me.

I put my headphones in, and the exact song I need to hear comes on—Wilco's "I Am Trying to Break Your Heart." I push play and close my eyes, and in one giant exhale I let the music wash over me. Of course, it was Amos who first introduced me to the album. It was a rainy Sunday last spring—gray days always make me moody for San Francisco—and I was half-heartedly attempting to distract myself from my homesickness with homework. I was sprawled out on the floor in Amos's room, writing my history paper on "Why Some Civilizations Advance" while he sorted through his record collection. Amos is meticulous about his records—he inherited most of them from his dad, and the rest he's acquired over the years, scavenging flea markets and record stores from Greenwich Village to Greenpoint.

"You've never heard *Yankee Hotel Foxtrot*?" he asked me, knowing that my music library consisted mostly of Top 40 and classical. I've loved music my entire life. And up until recently, playing piano was my absolute favorite thing to do. But it wasn't until Amos and I started hanging out that I realized I had been missing out on the good stuff. He introduced me to the greats.

I quickly closed my computer and lay down on the floor as Amos carefully took the record out of its sleeve. Even though he has the album on iTunes, Amos prefers to listen to everything on vinyl. He slowly dropped the needle down, and I smiled at the sound of the record crackling. He lay down on the floor next to me.

We listened to the whole record without saying a word. I felt hypnotized. I wasn't stoned, but I felt like I could be. It was like the music communicated everything I was feeling.

Amos started quietly singing along . . . and the thing was,

it sounded like he was singing to me. I could feel his breath in my ear, and we were looking right at each other. Suddenly, he jumped up, and turned the record player off.

"It stopped raining," he said, looking out the window. The sun was shining for the first time that day. "Hungry?" he asked, grabbing his keys.

We went out for Indian food, and as we walked home, the air smelled dewy and sweet. The lyrics from the album still echoed in my head—their honesty and their longing.

The car stops suddenly, and I'm brought back to reality. We've arrived at JFK. I put my phone in my bag, and as I get out of the car, Amos hands me my suitcase. He barely looks at me as he takes Poppy's hand and leads her into the airport.

9

POPPY

We're somewhere over Ohio, my eyes fixed on that little airplane icon inching across the screen on the seat back in front of me. I hate flying. And I stopped getting my preflight Benadryl when the recommended one-tablespoon dose stopped knocking me out and I started asking for more. Normally, I get so anxious I just try to sleep to avoid every awful second waiting until the plane lands. But not this time. This time, I'm watching that screen, hoping that for some magical reason, or maybe just because I want it bad enough, the plane will actually start flying backward. Then we can go back to New York, and things can stay the way they've always been.

I should be able to sleep right now, considering the fact that I never really fell asleep last night. Every time I closed my eyes, I had bad dreams—scared of what today would bring. My mind was spinning, trying to come up with some kind of way out, or at least around this disaster. If I could just delay it all for a few days. Or for forever.

"Why don't you turn that off?" Amos asks me for the fifth time. I know he's annoyed with me, but I can't help it. "Why don't we play a game? Go Fish?" he suggests. I love my brother so much, but he doesn't understand. No one does. Because they don't know what I know.

I turn and look out the window, even though I know I shouldn't. My stomach jumps into my throat, and for a second I think maybe it would be better if we just went down now. Then I wouldn't have to face what's to come. But then Mom and Dad would have to go to Ohio to identify our bodies after the crash. Mom hates Ohio and Iowa and Indiana and Nebraska. "Flyover states," she calls them. Places you fly over on your way to actual destinations, but would never want to go to. She got so mad when Dad wouldn't visit Grandma on the farm in Fairfield with her this past summer. It's something they've been fighting over lately. And by lately, I mean all the time.

It's weird how the things that my parents used to laugh about now blow up into humongo fights. Like, Dad used to joke around with Mom about how she has so many rules and opinions, like it was what made her special. And Mom used to always brag about how Dad worked so hard and was so important. But now it's like those are the things I hear them yelling about when it's late at night and they think I'm sleeping. I really hate it when anyone fights, but it's especially the worst when it's your very own parents. It feels so scary. How could two people who are supposed to love each other say such mean things?

But I'd give anything right about now to be back home, eavesdropping on their fights. Anything so that I'm back on solid ground. I have to stop catastrophizing—that's what Susan calls it when I tell her my fears in therapy. Mom just calls me "macabre." Suddenly there's a bump. I grab my brother's wrist, digging my jagged nails into his arms. I really need to start listening to Mom when she tells me not to bite them. So when Amos asks me again to watch a movie together, I agree.

FLYNN

Here we are, half an hour before we land in Los Angeles for our layover to Bora Bora, and we're still barely talking. This flight has felt like forever. I'm stuck sitting alone, while Amos and Poppy are across the aisle, watching a movie.

I can't help but laugh when I think about our Christmas trip last year. We were invited to stay at the Texas ranch of one of Louisa's top clients, Clint Holt. After two flights and a long, bumpy ride down a winding dirt road, we arrived—Louisa decked out in cowboy chic attire. The house was beautiful . . . that is, except for all the hunting trophies lining the walls. Everywhere you turned, there were sad deer eyes looking at you. Clint greeted us and introduced us to his wife, Christy, and their fifteen-year-old twins, Conner and Cody. "All *C*s! Isn't that the cutest?" Christy chirped as she clapped her hands together.

Amos, Poppy, and I took one look at Conner and Cody

with their mischievous grins and knew we were in trouble. When we went to bed that night, we found that they had short-sheeted our beds. From then on, the week was an all-out war of pranks between the Holts and the Abernathy-Barlows. At night, Poppy, Amos, and I would huddle together in my room and stay up planning how we'd get back at the Texas terrors. We'd barricade my door to ensure our safety, and all sleep together in the fort we built with every pillow and blanket we could find. That week ended up being the most fun we've ever had on a vacation. The way we all banded together, and how we'd laugh and laugh every night until we fell asleep.

The flight attendant asks me to buckle my seat belt, as the captain announces that we're preparing for our descent into the Los Angeles area. I look out my window at all the bright blue swimming pools below. I wonder which one belongs to Neel Khan. I haven't replied to his last few texts, if for no other reason than I really didn't know what else to say. I mean, he had a girlfriend all summer at camp who wasn't me. A girlfriend who happened to be Meredith, my best and oldest friend since elementary school. And sure, I thought he was flirting with me sometimes, and maybe I flirted back. But nothing ever happened. Because nothing ever happens. I'm just not that kind of girl.

Most of the junior counselors had been coming to camp since they were seven, including Meredith. Even though I'm not exactly the outdoorsy type, she convinced me that it would be fun to come back to California and spend the summer together. I hadn't been back since Mom died, but Meredith assured me that this was destined to be the Very Best Summer of Our Lives.

I spotted him on the first day. He was playing Ultimate Frisbee with a group of kids who looked like they were cut and pasted from a J.Crew catalog. But in the sea of sameness, Neel stood out. Not just because of his dark skin and deep brown eyes, thanks to his Indian roots, but because of his hipster style and infectious energy. I was sitting there with Meredith when I felt a thwack on my chest. It didn't take me long to register what had happened—unfortunately, I'm all too familiar with the feeling of volleyballs and the like hitting me in the face during mandatory PE at Spence.

The Frisbee in question was now lying at my feet, and all the players who I could already tell would be the "cool kids" of summer were standing there . . . watching me. Waiting for me to do something. Toss it back. Walk it over. Something. Anything. But I was paralyzed. Then I saw something kind in Neel's eyes.

"Sorry about that!" he called out. And in the warmth of his voice, I found the courage to reach down and throw the stupid Frisbee back. Somehow, it miraculously made it to him. "Nice pass," he said, flashing what I thought must be a million-dollar smile. "Come on! We're short a player!"

"Go on." Meredith nudged me, with a not-so-subtle wink. But I just continued to sit there, dumbstruck, my butt superglued to the ground. Neel had stalled the game, and now everyone was waiting for my response. After what felt like an eternity, Meredith hopped up and said, "All right. Then I'll go." And just like that, like it was happening in slow motion, I watched Meredith saunter onto the grass, with her short shorts and her blond hair swinging behind her. I couldn't believe how much Meredith had changed since her last visit to New York. Not only because her boobs had grown almost two sizes, but because she suddenly seemed so comfortable—with boys and, like, everything. I don't remember the rest of the game, but I do remember that Meredith and Neel made it to second base by midnight.

Like I said, I'm just not that kind of girl. At least, I don't think I am. But the thing is, recently, Neel and I have been texting all the time. We send each other funny memes, but we also just talk about our days. So even though last summer is long gone, I'm still replaying all the time I spent with him, feeling cursed by some lost chance. A chance that probably only existed in my imagination. Because, once again, I'm here—restless and unsettled—and I can't keep my thoughts or my feelings straight.

I've got to stop thinking about Neel. But I can't help it. What if I had joined the game instead of Meredith? What if, for once, I had stopped being so precious and scared, and had just acted on impulse? As the wheels touch down in Los Angeles, I wonder how far Malibu is from LAX.

AMOS

I'm lingering outside the ladies' room at LAX waiting for Flynn and Poppy. I swear, I feel like I could write the great American novel in the time I've spent waiting outside girls' bathrooms in this family. But we've got two hours before our next flight, and this place is a shit show. In the Christmas travel chaos there is not an empty seat in sight, so I throw my bag down and get comfortable sitting against what little wall space I can claim. I look around the airport, and I realize that the last time I was here, I was fourteen years old. My dad mixed up the flight times, so I had a few hours to kill before I left to go back to the city. He didn't bother to wait with me. Clay isn't that kind of dad. He isn't really much of a dad at all, which I guess is cool with me. It's weird now to think about a time when he and my mom were married. But I guess that was a time when he was a little more together, and she was a little less uptight.

That was when we were the Abernathys. We lived in the

West Village, and things were . . . easier. Louisa had a job at a small gallery in Chelsea, and Clay was always *not* working on something or other—a song, a poem, a painting. We were living what seemed to be the ideal faux-bohemian life, thanks to Clay's bottomless trust fund. Louisa and Clay were college sweethearts, or, rather, she studied at the University of Rhode Island while he was probably doing anything but studying at Brown. However different they were, however different the places they came from, I'd look at old pictures of them all young and artsy and think, *This is love.*

But all of that changed when Louisa got the job at Christie's. Suddenly, she cared that Clay never woke up before noon. Or that he'd started to paint a mural on their bedroom wall but never got around to finishing it. Or that he would fiddle around on his guitar until midnight. I don't blame her for having an affair with Jack. He's everything Clay's not. Jack's a self-made venture-capital gajillionaire from Silicon Valley. He's sensible and practical. Having an affair and getting Louisa pregnant is probably the one unstrategic thing he's ever done. But I know he felt like he was doing the most honorable thing under the circumstances by marrying her and moving to New York.

And so up we went to the Upper East Side. Clay headed out to California shortly after. I'd visit him during my school vacations, but you know how that goes. Christmas and Easter turn into just Christmas. That turns into every other Christmas. And then you realize you haven't seen your dad in years. The thing is, I hated going to see him anyway. At first it seemed cool—he was all hippied out, living in Venice Beach, letting me stay up super late and teaching me how to surf. But then it just got pathetic. Like how there was never any food in the fridge, or how there were always all these people just, like, hanging out at his house. He'd try to get all sentimental with me during those visits, but I'd just shrug when he asked me what my dreams were and shit. You want to know my dream, Clay? To turn out nothing like you.

Flynn and Poppy finally emerge from the restroom, debating how we should kill time during our layover, and I've gotta say, I'm relieved to have the distraction.

POPPY

We don't board our flight for Bora Bora for another two hours. Two hours! In two hours we could at least walk down Rodeo Drive, or cruise by the Hollywood sign to take a picture. In two hours we could do so many things. But instead we're sitting here, at LAX. It's so unfair—just out the window all of LA is waiting for me. It's so close, but so very far.

"We'd be back in time—I promise," I plead with Amos.

"No way. We're not leaving the airport," he says. And so I sigh, and get back to the Audrey Hepburn biography I'm reading. After all, I shouldn't be too surprised. The truth is, I get "no" a lot. No, Poppy, you can't sit with us at lunch today. No, Poppy, you can't stay home from school and watch old movies. No. No. No.

"Hey, look at those two," I say, as I point to a pair of old women in matching tracksuits and ginormous sunglasses. "I bet the one on the right—" But before I can finish, Amos puts his headphones on.

"Not now, Poppy."

I get up and sit next to Flynn. She's so pretty. I want to take a photo of her, but she doesn't look like she's in the mood. She seems kinda mad about something. So I tickle her arm because I know that it always makes her feel better. If I were pretty like Flynn, I'd always want people to photograph me. Instead I'm chubby and awkward, with eyes too far apart and a crooked smile. Rosie tells me it's what's on the inside that matters, and promises me that I'll have a growth spurt soon.

"Wouldn't it be fun to drive a bright red convertible up Pacific Coast Highway? We could have lunch in Malibu and pretend we're movie stars."

"We're close to Malibu?" Flynn perks up. She takes out her phone and looks like she's about to send a text, but then changes her mind. I want to ask her who she was going to text, but I know she won't tell me. When did we become a family with so many secrets?

I think about the secret I know. The biggest and only secret I've ever known. I want to tell them, but I don't think I'm supposed to. I look from Flynn to Amos and wonder what will happen to them—to us. And then my heart starts racing, and my thoughts are spinning around so fast it's making me dizzy. Will I ever see them again? Will they still love me? I just can't hold it in one minute, one second, longer.

"They're getting divorced," I blurt out. Flynn flinches, and Amos rips out his earphones. "They're planning on telling us in Bora Bora. It's supposed to be our last time together, as a family." And just saying it out loud makes my lip start to quiver.

The strange thing is, Flynn and Amos both just sit there for a minute, even more silent than they were before.

Finally Amos asks me, "Poppy, how do you know?"

"I'm home all the time. I hear things."

"What kind of things? Tell us exactly what you heard," Amos presses. I really hate being put on the spot.

"It was the middle of the night, and I couldn't sleep, so I went to their room. But I didn't go in because I could tell they were really mad about something by the way they were talking. At first I thought maybe it was about how Dad's been traveling so much lately. But Dad just kept saying, 'I can't keep doing this anymore. I'm done. It's over.' "

"Are you sure? I just don't understand—why would they trap us together on a boat in the middle of nowhere just to tell us that?" Flynn asks.

"They want it to be applicable."

"Amicable?" Amos corrects, as he struggles to make sense of it all.

"They have been fighting a lot," Flynn chimes in.

Amos turns to her accusingly. "Why didn't you say anything?"

"You haven't exactly been around these days." Flynn curls her legs into her chest, wraps her hands around her knees, and starts to rock back and forth like she does sometimes. "This can't be happening."

"Again," Amos adds. And then I remember that they've been through all of this before. With their first families. Their real families. But Flynn and Amos, they are my first family, my real family. My only family.

13

FLYNN

Amos takes Poppy's hands and kneels in front of her. "Poppy, are you sure they're planning to tell us when we get to Bora Bora?"

She nods, and I see a tear escape her left eye. "What's going to happen? What am I going to do without you guys?" she wonders.

My heart breaks. "Don't worry, Poppy. We're not going anywhere. We'll always have each other. You know that, right?" I wipe away her tears, trying to reassure her, even though I'm freaking out inside.

"But when Dad goes back to California—"

"What?" I snap, because *that* thought didn't occur to me. "He's moving? Poppy, is that what he said?"

"Yeah . . . I mean . . . I think so?" she says. "I heard Mom yelling about how she's tired of Dad complaining about New York all the time. And he said that maybe it would be better for him to spend more time at the Palo Alto office."

This isn't happening. My mind is flooded with a thousand questions. "But he wouldn't actually leave Poppy. Right?" I ask Amos imploringly, forgetting all our awkwardness for the moment.

"Well, he left you," Amos says. It stings, but he has a point there. Amos can sense I'm spiraling, because then he adds, "Whatever. Clay left me."

"So, dads just . . . leave?" Poppy asks. Neither of us knows how to answer.

And then the awful truth occurs to me. "If Dad is going back, that means I'll have to go, too." Everything is getting foggy.

"I don't want to go on this stupid trip," Poppy says.

We all sit there, reeling. "Then let's just not," I say.

"Not what?" Amos asks.

"Not go." I look at Amos, and then at Poppy. I stand up and grab my backpack. "F it."

I don't even know where the words are coming from. But I know if we don't move fast, I'll lose my nerve. We'll board the plane, and then get onto the boat, and then we'll be stuck—in the middle of the Pacific, and in the middle of Dad and Louisa's drama. All I know is that I can't lose Poppy and Amos—we're all we have.

"Get your stuff," I say, and after they do, I take their hands, pulling them up. Together we start running through the terminal. My feet return to their familiar rhythm, and there's only one thing I'm thinking . . .

Right-left-right-left-right-left.

POPPY

Ohmygosh ohmygosh ohmygosh ohmygosh ohmygosh ohmygosh ohmygosh ohmygosh

15

AMOS

And just like that we're running through LAX, holding each other's hands. I have no idea what the hell is going on, but I look at Poppy, squealing with delight as she tries to keep up, and then at Flynn, who's smiling for the first time since I've been home. Hearts pounding, we race down the escalator, weave through the carousels at baggage claim, and burst out the doors. And as we catch our breath at the curb, we're nearly blinded by the brightness of the LA sun. The blast of fresh air feels good, and there are palm trees swaying in the distance.

"Now what do we do?" Poppy asks.

"Whatever we want," Flynn answers with a mischievous grin I've never seen, and I can't help but laugh. Yeah, okay, Flynn. This stunt was a solid way to kill some time, but now the joke's over.

16

FLYNN

Amos is looking at me like I'm crazy. And who knows, maybe I am. But things seem clearer right here, right now, than they have in a long time. Because all I can think is . . . we're free.

"Can we go to Disneyland? Can we? Can we, please?" Poppy pleads.

"Of course," I say. "Where else? The beach? But we'll need bathing suits—"

"Hold up," Amos interrupts. "Flynn, you can't actually be serious right now."

How could I be anything but serious? My life is once again becoming a cross-country game of ping-pong. But before I can even respond, Amos just shakes his head and starts to walk back inside the airport. I run ahead of him, blocking his path.

"What are you doing?" I ask him.

"Well, first I'm going to wait in what I'm sure will be an

insanely long security line, then maybe I'll get a coffee, and then I'm going to get on our flight and go to Barbados like we're supposed to."

"It's Bora Bora, and don't ruin this. Please," I say.

"Flynn, there is no *this.* Do you really think we can just skip out on our flight and dick around LA without Jack and Louisa going ballistic? Have you even remotely thought this through?"

I look around at the cars and cabs crawling up the street, and the herds of tourists moving every which way, and I feel the momentum slipping away.

"Look," Amos continues, "I get it. The thought of Jack and Louisa giving us the 'it's not your fault' and 'we'll still be a family' talk makes me want to jump ship, too."

"So can't we just skip that part? It's not as if we're never going to go home. It's more like . . . we're just doing it on our own terms."

"You know they will freak out," he says.

"Since when do you care what other people think?"

Amos glances back at the airport's automatic doors opening and closing. Opening and closing.

"Please, Amos." Poppy pulls on his shirt. "If we don't get on that boat, it's like Mom and Dad aren't getting divorced. And then we can still stay . . . us."

"At least for a few more days," I add. "Can't we just . . . take a risk?"

Amos sighs and looks from me to Poppy, and then lovingly rubs the top of Poppy's head. "You know this is certifiably crazy?" he says. And without even thinking, I throw my arms around him. But as soon as I feel his chest against mine, my heart stops. We lock eyes for a second, and I don't even have to say thank you. I don't have to say trust me. He knows.

"So, we're fugitives. Now what?" he asks, his face fighting a smile. Poppy starts talking a mile a minute, listing all the sights she's desperate to see: the Sunset Strip, the Hollywood Hills, Rodeo Drive. It all sounds great—until we realize that we have no way of getting around.

"Well, what about . . ." I can't believe I'm even suggesting this.

"I'm not calling Clay."

"But—"

"Flynn. It's not happening." I can tell by his tone that this is nonnegotiable. And I get it. Even though we both know that we wouldn't have to worry about Clay ratting us out to Louisa, given the fact that they've basically vowed to never speak to each other ever again.

"Let's rent a convertible! A red one," Poppy pipes in.

"We're too young to rent a car. You have to be twenty-five. So, Flynn, I don't know how you plan on us actually going anywhere."

"I know someone who has a car," I say. As I take out my phone, Amos snatches it from me.

"You make a terrible fugitive. If you really want to do this right, we have to be smart about it. Use that thing, and they'll track us down before you can say Amber Alert."

That's when I realize that, despite everything, Amos wants to be here.

"You're right," I say. "No phones. No credit cards. No

trace." We dig into our bags and walk over to the garbage can outside the terminal.

"And to think I just got to the next level on Minecraft," Poppy says as she wistfully looks at her phone. "Oh well." She grins from ear to ear.

"So we're doing this." I look at Amos and Poppy.

And then, without saying anything else, we toss our phones into a trash can outside the Los Angeles International Airport. We're officially off the grid.

17

AMOS

Divorce. Again. Statistically, it's impressive Jack and Louisa even lasted this long, considering their prior history of commitment issues. And how they've always found a way to bitch about everything—like how Jack refuses to take his shoes off in the house, and how Louisa is just so *Louisa.* And let's not forget about all the fights they have about Poppy. One thing's for sure, there is no way I am ever getting married. What's the point? So I can make a bunch of promises I'll inevitably break? No thanks.

Poppy, Flynn, and I are walking in search of a pay phone, something that is proving to be harder to find than one would imagine. There used to be pay phones on every corner—or so Louisa says whenever she reminisces about a time before smartphones—an Eden without selfie sticks and idiots getting run over texting while crossing the street. Well, where the hell did all these alleged pay phones go? It turns out life without Google Maps, or Uber, or any connection to the outside world, is a bit more complicated than we anticipated. And slow. The utter absurdity of this situation seems to only increase with each step we take away from the airport, with only our carry-on backpacks in tow.

If only I'd known, when I walked out of our apartment and left for school back in August, that I would be walking out of my old life forever. I was so happy to leave that space, those walls, those memories. But now there won't be any more memories to make. Not at 77 East Seventy-Third at least. It's just messed up. Because even though Jack and Louisa fight, they're still Jack and Louisa. Sure, they sometimes seem more like business partners than parents. But they are our parents nonetheless.

And what if Poppy's got this all wrong? She's just a kid. Kids get confused all the time. But kids also pick up on the slightest things—the nuanced changes that parents stupidly think they're too young to notice. I remember those middle-of-the-night fights Louisa and Clay used to have—I'd crawl out of bed and stand in the hallway in my Batman pj's, holding my breath, terrified they would catch me eavesdropping. Kids know. And Poppy's no ordinary kid.

Not to mention, I did think something was up when Louisa was hosting all those dinner parties last spring. Louisa's events are always somewhat of a circus. The raison d'être for the occasion is usually the arrival of an artist from abroad—and recently, one artist in particular. Hans Gleitman is, according to Louisa, a charismatic and *very* important artist. The hours leading up to her dinners are a flurry of activity: deliveries of white flowers from Belle Fleur (anemones in winter, peonies in spring, and lilies in between) and cases of wine and booze from Sherry-Lehmann. Rosie reluctantly and territorially presides over the catering staff in the kitchen, and tries to put Poppy into whatever party dress Louisa has picked out for the occasion. Meanwhile, Louisa stomps around, goading Jack, Flynn, and me to get dressed, approving and disapproving of outfits and hairstyles along the way.

When the guests arrive, cocktails and hors d'oeuvres are served in the living room. We kids are expected to attend, not so much to engage in conversation, but to sit there and look a certain way. As if we're another bouquet dropped off by the florist. And then every so often Louisa trots us out like little show ponies, requesting a piano solo from Flynn, or signaling me to recall an author or artist that "slipped her mind." Flynn and I are convinced it's an act, though. Things like that don't exactly slip Louisa's mind. She straight-up seizes the opportunity to demonstrate her son's knowledge of the arcane information she deems valuable. Like it's some reflection on her.

When Poppy was younger, Louisa would let her put on little performances in the living room. Poppy would dress up in her pink tutu or her tap shoes and fumble through whatever routine she was learning in the dance classes Louisa made Rosie drag her to. But I guess at some point, Poppy's lack of balletic talent became more apparent, and Louisa found that less than adorable. So recently, Louisa deemed the dinners "adults only." Flynn and I were still expected to attend, while little Poppy was left to eat alone at the kitchen counter with Rosie. That's when Flynn and I decided to rebel. We conspired to sabotage wherever we could—to show the cracks in Louisa's carefully constructed façade of the perfect family.

It's a scheme Flynn and I found especially entertaining whenever Hans was in town. We'd slip some extra salt into whatever was simmering in the chafing dish, or accidentally spill something onto the white Alexander McQueen dress that Louisa had poured herself into. We would come up with outrageous opinions to share too vocally along with insidious examples of Louisa's poor parenting.

Now that I think about it, Jack was noticeably absent at the last few dinner parties. Kinda makes me wonder . . .

We finally find a pay phone outside a gas station, and Flynn picks up the receiver.

"Who do you even know in Los Angeles?" I ask.

"My friend Neel. We met last summer at camp."

Interesting. Our detour is suddenly making a lot more sense.

"What's he, like your summer crush?" I ask.

"We're just . . . friends." But I can tell by her tone, and the way she's avoiding eye contact with me, that she's lying. Flynn is good at a lot of things, but lying is not one of them. Deceit and manipulation don't come naturally to her—which is probably why she hasn't had the easiest time navigating high school.

"How convenient," I respond. After a few minutes Flynn hangs up and informs us that this Neel person is going to meet us at the giant doughnut nearby. Could things get any more surreal? We walk for what feels like an hour.

"Are we there yet?" Poppy whines hungrily. I take her

backpack off her shoulders to lighten her load. And there in the distance, like a mirage, is a giant doughnut looming in the sky. Our stomachs all let out a collective grumble.

"Can we get one?" Poppy asks.

"Of course," I say, before realizing that I'm not even sure how much cash I have on me. Shit. "How much money do you have?" I ask Flynn. She takes out her wallet and I do the same. Poppy pulls out a twenty-dollar bill that Louisa makes her keep in her backpack for emergencies. I count the money. Together we have $164.35. It's not a lot, but hey, at least doughnuts are cheap.

FLYNN

Amos orders an iced coffee (black, of course), and then gives Poppy a few dollars. He steps aside to let her deliberate about which doughnuts to choose from the display. He wordlessly offers me the caffeinated beverage, and I take a long sip from the plastic straw. The coffee is strong, and I feel it trickle down into my empty stomach. I take another sip and then pass it back to him.

"Thanks," I say. "I needed that."

"Figured it was worth the two dollars."

"It's not as good as Kyong's, but what is?" I say, referring to the coffee we used to get every morning from the bodega on our block. But Amos just looks like he's thinking about something else.

"Divorce . . . shit. That's a hell of a birthday present," he says to me.

"I thought it wasn't possible to hate my birthday any more than I already do."

"Do you think it was an affair?" Amos asks.

"What?"

"The demise of our parents' marriage."

"Oh. I hadn't gotten that far," I reply.

"You know, Louisa did spend a lot of time in Amagansett this summer," he offers.

"So you're saying . . ."

"I'm saying, a lot of weekends turned into ten-day stays."

It's not like she hasn't cheated before, I think.

"And it's not like she hasn't cheated in the past," Amos says, thinking the same thing.

"Well, the same goes for my dad," I say, but for some reason it's harder to imagine him having another affair.

Amos shakes his head. "Nah, it wasn't Jack. No one would want to face the wrath of Louisa for something like that," he says with certainty. Amos has this ability to just know things about other people. Like everyone's inner lives and secrets are just so obvious. He's quiet for a moment. "Do you think it was—" he starts to say, but just then Poppy comes over with a brown bag already stained with doughnut grease.

"Do you think what?" she asks innocently.

Amos and I grasp for straws. "Do you think you got enough?" I cover. And then Amos playfully snatches the bag from Poppy. We'll save the rest of this conversation for a Poppy-free zone. She doesn't need to know all the dirty details. At least we can spare her that.

POPPY

I lick the sticky icing off my fingers as I finish my second glazed doughnut. Sure, my stomach hurts a little (okay, a lot) from the sugary goodness, but back home Mom would never let me overdose on sweets like this. And definitely not this early in the day. As instructed, every morning Rosie makes me scrambled eggs (one yellow, two whites) and gluten-free toast, Monday through Friday. And as instructed, I take my two little white pills, Monday through always. Susan says to think of taking my pills like brushing my teeth. Like it or not, it's just something I have to do.

It hasn't always been two white pills. There have been blue pills, and pink pills, and for a while I was taking up to four different ones a day. Some of them would make me sleepy, and some of them would make me so hyper, it was like I'd had six Shirley Temples in a row. Mom says it's such a relief that we've finally found the right dose for me. I guess I feel relieved about it, too. I just want to feel normal.

Wait! My pills. Where did we put them? Uh-oh. I unzip the front pocket of my backpack, but all that's inside is a very, very brown banana. Ick. I close my eyes and try to remember everything Rosie and I packed yesterday. We carefully placed my underwear, and pj's, and the new one-piece bathing suits Mom got me, in the suitcase. And then we put in my toiletry case, and zipped everything up. My toiletry case—with my toothbrush and toothpaste and retainers and nose spray and all the rest of my medicine. Which means my pills—the pills I take at breakfast time and bedtime—are on their way to Bora Bora. I feel sweaty.

"You guys?" I look at my brother and sister, my voice shaking.

"Yeah, Pops?" Flynn ruffles my hair.

But then I realize—if I tell them about my missing medicine, they'll make me go back to the airport and this will all be over. "I—I forgot what I was gonna say," I stammer. I took them this morning. I'll be okay. I'm sure of it. I know Mom and Dad and Rosie are going to be mad, but this is my family, too, and don't I get a say on whether we all stay together? It's not fair for them to just pull us apart. I need us together. Whatever it takes.

"Your friend Neel is taking his sweet time," Amos says to Flynn as he gets up from the curb. Earlier, Amos asked Flynn if Neel is her boyfriend, and she said no. But it sounds like maybe he is. Or maybe she wants him to be. Flynn smiles as a black SUV pulls up. Neel leans out the window and smiles at us. He is so cute, and not at all like the boys in the city. And now I get why Flynn wants him to be her boyfriend.

FLYNN

"Barlow," he says with a slight smile.

"Khan," I reply, trying desperately to keep my cool. Amos, Poppy, and I quickly hop into Neel's Land Rover, as if Dad and Louisa were actually on our tail. I slide into the front seat, and I can't decide if I'm supposed to hug Neel. Instead I just buckle up. I look over at him and realize how utterly strange it is seeing Neel outside camp—outside the only context we have for each other. It's not as if I haven't wondered what his life is like out here in Los Angeles. I've spent more time than I'd ever like to admit scrolling through the filtered photos on his Instagram feed. And now here I am, sitting in his car. No filters. Just Neel—in swim trunks, a faded blue T-shirt, and slip-on sneakers. With his messy hair and easy smile. I immediately remember what drew me to him. And suddenly I feel . . . nervous.

"You're rolling deep," he says as he gestures to Amos and Poppy in the backseat.

"Oh, sorry," I say. "Neel . . . this is Amos and Poppy. Amos, Poppy . . . this is Neel." Poppy slides down her cat-eye sunglasses and dangles her hand out, as if she were a movie star from another era.

"Pleasure to meet you, darling," she says in her best grown-up voice. I'm nervous Neel won't play along, but luckily, it seems like he remembers everything I've already told him about Poppy.

Without missing a beat he replies, "And where might I take you today, young lady?"

"Beverly Hills! Where else?"

"You got it."

Neel speeds up. We have an entire glorious day before we're supposed to arrive in Bora Bora—before Jack and Louisa even realize we're missing. I roll down my window and hold out my arm, caressing the gentle breeze. This morning in Manhattan feels like a lifetime ago. The snow and skyscrapers have morphed into sunshine and strip malls. Even though I grew up in Northern California, I've never really been to Los Angeles. As I look out the window, I can't tell if this city is ugly or beautiful or both.

I catch my reflection in the rearview mirror, my hair back and my face bare—my hangover from last night still clearly hanging over me. I curse myself for snoozing through my alarm so many times this morning. At least I brushed my teeth. Any reasonable girl would have at least put some makeup on while we were waiting for Neel, but the trouble is, all my toiletries are en route to Bora Bora.

All I've got with me are the contents of my overstuffed backpack: *Billy Budd* (school reading), *East of Eden* (me reading), Sour Patch Kids, Aquaphor, my Warbys, and a scarf. I look down at my gray T-shirt, black skinny jeans, and white Converse—my unofficial uniform as of late. Not my best look, but I guess not my worst, either. Like I said, I overslept. Not to mention, I didn't exactly plan on seeing Neel Khan today. I pull my hair out of a braid and run my fingers through its dark brown waves. It's so long these days Poppy says I look like a mermaid.

Amos, slouched in the seat behind me, catches me fidgeting in the mirror. He's been silent since we got in the car. I hope he's not regretting this. But then again, anyone with some semblance of sanity would probably be questioning what in the world we're doing here. In Los Angeles. In Neel Khan's car.

I mean, what *are* we doing here? How well do I even know Neel? I've watched enough *Dateline* to know that there are a lot of ways this could go. Okay, maybe I'm being a bit dramatic, but the reality is, we are going to have to go home eventually. And eventually I'm going to have to admit that this whole crazy thing was my idea.

But then I look over at Neel, and he's even cuter than I remember. And I know that whatever is happening here, in this car, is right. It's like I've been researching risk my whole life, and it finally feels like it's time to let go and just be fearless for a little while.

"I can't believe you guys ran away. That's pretty baller,"

Neel says. "Didn't know you had it in you." I smile, hoping he means that as a compliment. "So does this mean I'm considered an accomplice?" he asks.

"That all right with you?" I say, trying to sound like this all isn't the biggest deal in the world. The thing I always liked about Neel was how unserious he seemed. But not in an uninteresting way. It's like he knows how messed up the world is but he isn't going to let it get in his way. Neel's dad is some big Bollywood movie producer, and his stepmom is his Swedish former au pair. "A true LA story," as he calls it. His dad is always traveling back to Mumbai, and it sounds like now that she's off the clock, the last thing his stepmom is interested in is looking after him. So Neel's alone a lot, like me. But he doesn't seem bothered by it. He says it's freeing—like not having his parents around is maybe even a good thing.

On my first day off from camp last summer, I wandered around the small hick town just north of Yosemite. There wasn't much to see, so I finally sat down on a bench, exasperated and annoyed. And then I just started crying. Because the last time I had been to Yosemite I'd probably been Poppy's age, and I'd been with my mom. And sometimes, the memories and the grief—it all feels like too much. Because I miss my mom in a way that's hard to understand, and most of the time even harder to feel. But it's there—the missing. It doesn't go away, and maybe I don't even want it to.

As I was sitting there on the bench, quietly crying to myself, someone suddenly sat down next to me. It was Neel. He said he was in the mood for a snack, so I suggested ice cream, and then off we went. We spent the rest of the afternoon walking in the woods, and I tried not to feel like the worst person in the world because, in my head, I was pretending that Neel wasn't my best friend's boyfriend. I pretended that he was my boyfriend.

Eventually we had to head back to camp, and just as we were about to walk into the mess hall, Neel stopped and looked at me. I held my breath, and wondered if he was going to kiss me. He leaned in, and then paused. "You know, you're the coolest girl here, Barlow," he said with a smile. And before I could even respond, he opened the door, and we were flooded with all the noise and chaos of dinner. Meredith waved us over, and as I watched Neel sit down and put his arm around her, everything I hoped we'd shared that afternoon melted away.

The strange thing is, even when he was dating Meredith, I felt somehow that there was something between Neel and me. Or maybe it was all in my head. It's just that I need to believe someone else is out there who gets me. Someone more simple, less complicated. Someone . . . other than him.

"Turn up the tunes!" Poppy commands from the backseat. Neel and I both reach for the volume, and our hands touch. His fingers linger on mine. Or maybe I imagine that part. But either way, it feels . . . electric.

21

AMOS

I should have just said no. But it was all happening so fast, and she was standing there, with her *Please don't disappoint me, Amos* eyes, and the only thing I could say was yes. I catch Flynn's eye in the rearview mirror, and then look away. Even though I try not to think about it, I know how much I've disappointed her.

I should have told her I was leaving. But all summer in Amagansett, it was like every time I sat down to write her a real email, or at least something other than a reply-all to the latest from Poppy, I'd let myself get distracted with anything and everything. I'd stay out too late at a bonfire looking for girls to make out with, or lose myself in a long sail along the sound. Because every time I tried to tell her why I was leaving, it felt like a lie.

And so I went away to look for the truth. I felt this need

to get out of town—to leave the city behind. It was time to simplify. I was leaving a lot: I'd been friends with some of these guys since we were practically preschoolers, and we were finally going to be upperclassmen. I'd also earned a starting spot on varsity lacrosse for my junior year, which was no small feat. But life is full of leaving people behind—or being left behind.

I'm sure the kids at Andover think I'm weird, and I don't blame them. I'm the guy who showed up on their revered campus and couldn't give a shit. They're all rah-rah, bowing down to their hallowed halls like they're in some cult. Like they need to make sure their high school experience is everything they've been told it should be. To be honest, it's kind of nice being the outsider. I don't have to pretend to care about their private jokes, and they certainly don't have to worry about filling me in on the latest gossip, or saving a seat for me in Paresky Commons. I've become friends with a few of the international kids, and other than smoking the occasional joint with them, I spent most of first semester studying. To be honest, I'm usually happy wandering the five hundred acres of perfectly groomed lawns with just me and my thoughts. I've been reading a lot of David Foster Wallace, and trust me, that guy has a lot more to say about life than most kids at that school.

Tryouts are coming up for lacrosse, and I'm looking forward to getting back out on the field. They'll make me pay my dues, that's for sure, but I don't mind a little grit. A coach from Brown has already contacted me to say he'd like to come see me play once the season starts. I know I should be excited about it (Louisa certainly is), but I feel like I'm in no place to decide anything. How the hell am I supposed to choose a path, and charge full speed ahead, when I have no clue where I'm actually going?

And now, here we are in LA, heading who knows where. I don't know what the deal is with Flynn and this dude, but I already know I don't like him. He's driving around like he owns this town, and for all I know, maybe he does. I'm trying not to watch them up front playing with the radio. I'm really just along for the ride. I feel like I owe it to her. Because the truth—the real truth—is that I left New York because of Flynn.

POPPY

This is the best day ever! Flynn's friend Neel is taking us on a driving tour of Beverly Hills, and honestly, it's everything I hoped it would be. Except it's not very hilly. The houses are huge, and every one is a different style. There's this one that looks like an actual witch's house, and one that looks like it was made out of toothpaste, and Neel even showed us where Jennifer Lawrence lives. Oh! And then there's this one humongo house on Sunset Boulevard, where the whole front yard is full of giant Santa Clauses!

There are reindeer jumping across the street in front of Saks Fifth Avenue, which isn't even on Fifth Avenue here. It's on Wilshire. Next to the real Regent Beverly Wilshire, from one of my all-time favorite movies, *Pretty Woman.* Neel also showed us the fountain from *Clueless,* the one Cher walks by in the super-sad montage. And Phyllis Nefler's house from *Troop Beverly Hills.* All the landmarks, really. There are guys on the street selling star maps, and I beg Amos to buy me one, but he says we have to draw the line somewhere.

It's kind of funny seeing all the holiday decorations and lights, because it doesn't feel like Christmas at all here. Maybe because of all the palm trees. Or maybe because from the backseat, I can see that Neel's car says it's eighty-two degrees outside.

Flynn reaches over and takes Neel's sunglasses off, and puts them on. Amos rolls down his window, and the warm air feels so good that even he relaxes. Why doesn't everyone live in LA? Maybe I can get Mom and Dad to move here instead of getting divorced. Then maybe Amos will come live with us again. And then maybe Flynn will be happy again. I can't imagine anyone could ever be unhappy in California. Whatever we do, we have to find a way to stay together—to stay us.

FLYNN

Neel parks his Land Rover on a side street off Sunset Boulevard. We unload, and follow him down a pink path lined with palm fronds, and Poppy is practically frothing at the mouth as he leads us the "back way" into the mythic Beverly Hills Hotel. He sure knows the way to that girl's heart. The air smells like flowers, fancy perfume, and maple syrup. An older man in a sports coat opens the door for his much younger companion, impeccably clad in a white suit. *Definitely mistress,* I say, but only to myself. I hear the faint sound of a piano coming from the restaurant. It's typical hotel music—Frank Sinatra or something. It's supposed to be lovely and benign, but I can't help but be bothered by it. I wonder if I'll ever want to play again. As we walk in from the side entrance, I look at our grubby airplane clothes.

"Are we dressed okay?" I ask Neel.

"We're not eating up here," he says, as he guides us past

the Polo Lounge, and continues to a staircase just beyond the restaurant. He takes the steps two at a time, as if it's his own house. As we descend, we all steal a glance through a window, beyond which is a fifties-style coffee shop.

"Did you *see* that?" Poppy cries. "Taylor Swift is sitting at the counter!"

"No she isn't," Amos scoffs.

"Yeah, it was definitely her!"

"It wasn't," he snips. Well, it's good to know Amos still takes pleasure in being such a contrarian.

We follow Neel past the gift shop, hair salon, and spa and out the back doors. He leads us down another set of stairs, and straight past a sign that says HOTEL GUESTS ONLY, to the swimming pool. The pool itself is massive. The water is the brightest blue, and the green-and-white-striped lounge chairs contrast perfectly with the pink backdrop of the hotel. It is quintessential Beverly Hills.

Neel goes over to the hostess, who looks barely older than we are. They exchange a few words I can't quite hear, and then she escorts us to a row of cabanas on the far wall. I don't need to turn my head to know that Amos and Neel are transfixed watching her impossibly short white tennis skirt graze the top of her perfectly toned and tan thighs. I pull at my T-shirt, thinking of my own vampire-pale skin, and for a split second wonder what I'm doing here.

"You have your pick today," she chirps, and Neel turns to me to make the call.

"Ummm . . ." I scan the nearly empty row of cabanas, and Poppy pipes in, "That one!"

"You heard the lady," Neel tells the hostess. She giggles, and tells us she'll be back with some menus. And maybe I'm imagining this, but she may have even winked.

The hostess returns a minute later with menus and more witty banter. She somehow manages to flirt with friendly nonchalance, and I wonder if they teach that at whatever junior college she goes to.

"Can I get a hamburger?" Poppy asks. It takes Amos and me a second to realize that she's talking to us—because to her, we're the adults here. Amos and I look at each other—both knowing full well that Louisa's answer would be unequivocally *no.*

"Sure, Poppy," Amos acquiesces. So he's playing it like that. Poppy is on a special diet. Louisa claims it's because gluten aggravates her condition, but Amos and I have always suspected that Louisa's just so vain that she can't handle the thought that her precious daughter wasn't blessed with her flawless frame. Either way, I'm not going to let Amos be the only good guy here, so when Poppy says, "And fries," and looks at me, I nod.

"These prices are steep—we have to share," Amos says as he takes a closer look at the menu. "We've only got a hundred and fifty-nine dollars left."

"And twenty-three cents," Poppy adds.

"Don't worry, bro," Neel says. "I got this."

"It's fine. I'm not that hungry anyway," he replies. Seriously? Is Amos really so stubborn that he would rather starve than owe Neel money?

"C'mon, Amos. We need to save what we can," I say, wondering how far we really can make it without the safety of Dad and Louisa's bank account.

"Fine, but we're going to pay you back. Eventually," Amos says to Neel.

"Sure, man. No worries," Neel says.

"So does that mean I can get a milk shake, too?" Poppy asks.

"Now you're pushing it . . . but okay, just don't tell Mom," Amos says, giving in. And we can't help but smile.

AMOS

Don't be that girl, I think as Flynn salivates over that douchebag Neel Khan and picks at her twenty-seven-dollar Caesar salad (which, for the record, I'll pay him back for). She's changing, I can tell. I know I've only been gone a few months, but something's shifted. She's more withdrawn, and at the same time clearly trying so hard to be noticed. Like she's got something to prove. Some kind of agenda. Just like everybody else. C'mon, Flynn, don't be like everybody else.

Last night Rosie mentioned she'd stopped playing piano, too, which is insane, considering that she used to practice for so many hours a day it almost sounded strange in the apartment when it was just plain old quiet. When Flynn first moved in, I could tell she was self-conscious about practicing when Poppy or I was home. But eventually, she started playing more and more. I didn't want her to feel nervous, or like she had an audience, so I would pretend to get a snack, and just linger in the kitchen so I could really hear her. Man, can she play. Sure, she practiced all the time, but it was something more than that—real talent, I guess. Soon enough, Poppy started making requests: everything from show tunes to Selena Gomez. Louisa is practically already filling out Flynn's Juilliard application for her, which is certifiable since she's only a sophomore, but still, Flynn would be stupid to give it up.

And what's with this running thing? Flynn's always been allergic to exercise. It's like she's philosophically opposed to the whole idea. She's always been more . . . lethargic. Like a house cat. While all the other girls on the Upper East Side were starving themselves into their skinny jeans and SoulCycling their Saturdays away, we would park ourselves on the couch and binge on good doughnuts and bad TV. Our marathon sofa sessions were epic, and one of the things I missed most at boarding school.

When I'd think about those memories, I'd look around my dorm room—the white walls empty, the navy sheets balled up on my twin bed—and everything would just feel too quiet. That's when I would text Mia. I wouldn't even have to wait for a response. She'd just be there, at my door. We pretty much hooked up all of fall semester. I could tell from the first time I saw her that Mia's the kind of girl who doesn't give a shit. She knows all the kids at school have about a million and one theories about all those scars on her body. But she walks around like she doesn't owe anybody anything. And I've got to admit, it's pretty hot.

I guess you could say we're "friends with benefits"—except we're not really friends. We barely say hi when we pass each other in the West Quad in between classes, but that's fine with me. Mia isn't asking me to like her, isn't asking me to need her. And she knows the same goes for me. Not everything has to be so complicated.

I lie back on the lounge and let myself feel the heat of the sun, grateful to be away from the bitter cold of school and the crazy of the city. But then my mind wanders back to what will happen when we don't step off that plane in Bora Bora. Jack and Louisa will lose their shit, and poor Rosie back home will be hysterical. But then there's a giant splash, and suddenly I'm soaked in water. The kid cannonballed into the pool right in front of me.

"Barlow, get your ass in here!" Neel calls out to Flynn.

"I don't have a bathing suit," she says coyly, and I think I could be sick. I watch as she gets up and delicately dips her toe in the pool.

"Just wear your bra and underwear," he goads. And from the way she's biting her lower lip, I can tell that she's actually considering it. "Why not? It's practically the same thing," the perv says, continuing to pressure her.

"Do it!" Poppy cajoles.

"Flynn," I retort.

"Can I go in, too?" Poppy persists.

"No. No one's going in the pool," I say, sounding like a father, just no father I ever had. "Besides, don't you have to wait like thirty minutes after eating, or something?"

But Flynn doesn't even look back at me. She just peels off her T-shirt and jeans. I feel like I should look away, but I can't avert my eyes. I've never seen Flynn in her underwear before. She dives in, and finally I can breathe again.

25

FLYNN

Swoooooosh. I let myself sink to the bottom, and just stay there. Sinking. It's so quiet and still—like a womb. I hold my breath until I feel like I'm going to burst, and then, *swoooosh,* I push myself back up. It's bright and loud again, and as I catch my breath, my eyes refocus, and I see that Neel and I are standing face to face.

"Hey," I manage to say, despite my panting. He steps closer to me. Now we're nose to nose. But before I even have time to figure out what's behind his smile, he splashes me. "Hey!" I shout, as I splash him right back. As I try to swim away, he grabs my arm. His grip feels good, strong. I look down at my polka-dot bra and striped underwear and pretend that I don't care that he's seeing me like this, even though I totally do. Neel ducks his head back underwater and swims off to the deep end—he moves so gracefully, I can see why he's the star of his school's water polo team. His back looks like a sculpture, the muscles taut and distinct.

I wonder how many girls Neel has hooked up with. Probably a lot. It wouldn't be hard for most people to have more experience than I've had (a few make-outs, most of which were during Truth or Dare and hardly count). I don't know why I've been such a prude my whole life, or what I'm really waiting for. Even the idea of hooking up with random guys has always made me feel kind of sad. Not that I'm some romantic sap. It just seems sort of strange to be that reckless with your emotions.

But now it's as if everyone around me is not only making out, but, you know, doing more than that, too. Like it was some assignment over summer vacation for every girl at Spence to have sex. Literally. It's all anyone talked about the whole month of September—suddenly there was a divide between the girls who have done it and those who haven't. I never even asked Meredith if she and Neel went all the way. I think she thought it was because I was secretly judging her, but really it was because I was jealous. I worry what Meredith would think about me being half-naked in the pool with Neel right now, but she broke up with him and already has a new boyfriend.

I'm not really sure what to do with Neel just, like, looking at me, so I duck back underwater and swim over to the ledge by Poppy and Amos. "Come in, Pops!" I call out. I don't even bother asking Amos, because I can't stand the thought of him rolling his eyes at me one more time today. I don't know why I need his approval. Or why even though I'm mad and hurt and confused, I'm still happy we're here, in Los Angeles . . . together.

26

POPPY

If Flynn's in her underwear, I guess it's okay that I'm in mine, too. I pull at my undershirt as I sit on the steps of the pool. I lower myself down one more. Now my legs are fully underwater. I think about going down one step farther, but maybe I'll stay here another minute longer.

Some French kids who look about my age race past me and jump right into the pool, like it isn't the biggest deal in the whole world. I tell myself to just breathe in slowly . . . and out slowly. In . . . and . . . out. Susan tells me to do this when my mind starts speeding super fast. Sometimes when I'm at school, I feel like I could just scream. Like, there was this one time last year, I got back to the classroom a few minutes late from recess, and when I sat down at my desk, I knew something was different. My box of pens is always, *always* on the top right corner, and my mini pack of Kleenex is always,

always on the top left corner. I keep my two sharpened pencils that Mac gives me from the Carlyle in the drawer below, right next to my Paddington Bear ruler. I know I'm way too old for Paddington, but Rosie gave it to me for my birthday, and Flynn says it's the thought that counts.

I like having everything on my desk a certain way. When everything is in order, it just makes more sense, you know? But when I got back from recess, I saw that my box of pens was in my desk, my Kleenex were all crumpled up, and my pencils and eraser were missing. I felt like I was choking or something because it was getting really hard for me to breathe. I looked around at the other kids, and they all just sat there, pretending not to watch me, pretending not to laugh.

Then Ms. Friedman came in, and when she asked me to sit down, my body froze. All the kids started really laughing, and Ms. Friedman walked over to me and asked me what was wrong. But when she saw my desk, she knew. It wasn't like this was the first time. She took me to the attendance office and I texted Amos, and twenty-seven minutes later he was there. By then it was lunchtime, so he sat with me on the playground, and we shared the sushi and edamame Rosie had packed for me. He had to go back to Collegiate to take a chemistry quiz, but I promised him I'd be okay for the rest of the day. And the thing is, I was.

Sometimes I wonder what it would be like to be the same as the other kids. The way they can run around on the playground even when their shoes are untied. Or how the other girls can just sit together at lunch—laughing and telling secrets. But whenever I try to get the guts to go up and talk to them, I think about all the times they've laughed at me, and I just feel safer staying right where I am.

Flynn swims over, takes my hand, and leads me off the steps and into the water. "One, two, three!" she says, and we dunk our heads. And it's not a big deal at all. I can't believe I was wasting all that time, waiting on the steps. We do handstands together, and see who can hold her breath the longest, and even though our fingers are starting to look like prunes, there is no way I'm ever getting out.

Neel catches Flynn by surprise and lifts her up on his shoulders. She screams out a little too loudly, I guess, because a hotel employee comes over and asks for our room number. Neel says we're not guests, and the man tells us in a super-serious voice that we need to leave the property immediately. Flynn kicks Neel, and he lowers her down. I just stay perfectly still. I really hate getting in trouble.

But Neel doesn't seem freaked out at all. He just calmly brushes back his black hair, and tells the man that he must be new at the hotel because they haven't met yet, and that he's sure that if they had, he would know who Neel's dad is. And then it's the weirdest thing—because the guy from the hotel starts apologizing to us! He's all, "I'm so sorry, Mr. Khan." He asks if we could use some more towels or anything else, but Neel looks at Flynn and says, "No worries, man. We were just leaving, right?" And Flynn nods and takes my hand, and off we go.

FLYNN

I pull my wet hair back into a ponytail with the thin black rubber band that is always around my wrist. My skin smells like chlorine, like summer. We're back on the road, heading to see the Hollywood sign (per Poppy's request), but first we have to go pick up a friend of Neel's at some sneaker store.

"Pull over!" Poppy hollers from the backseat.

I whip around. "What's wrong?"

"Look! The lights!" she says, pointing out her window. I look across the street and see the giant structures that make up the Los Angeles County Museum of Art. Perched in front is an installation of rows and rows of old streetlights.

"We have to stop!" Poppy insists.

"I don't think we have time for a museum right now," I tell her.

"It's better at night when it's all lit up anyway," Neel adds.

"But it's an LA landmark. I see it all over Instagram. I just need one photo. Pretty please?" she begs.

"Do you mind?" I ask Neel.

"How about this," he says as he makes a U-turn, and pulls up in front of the museum. "I'll drive around the block, you guys get your photo on, and meet back here."

"I promise we'll be quick!" I say, as Poppy, Amos, and I jump out of the car. We run up to the exhibit, and weave through the lampposts. It's super crowded with couples taking cheesy selfies and kids running around in circles. And somehow, despite the fact that lampposts are really so ordinary, there's something enchanting about the exhibit. Poppy instructs me to twirl around a post *Singin' in the Rain*–style while she snaps a Polaroid.

Suddenly, Amos jumps out from behind a lamp. "You're it!" he yells, tagging Poppy, and runs off. I try to escape, but Poppy gets me quickly, and races away. I look around for Amos, but he seems to have disappeared in the mix. Suddenly, I spot him from behind, and I stealthily slink over, and tap him on the shoulder.

"Got you!" I scream, and run off before he can catch me.

The three of us have spent a lot of time running around museums and being around art. While most New York families spend their Sunday mornings at brunch, the Abernathy-Barlows can be found at galleries and museums all over the city. Louisa says it's good *exposure.* Sometimes Louisa invites Amos and me to the fancy opening parties. I don't know why she thinks it's appropriate for us to be there among all the adults, but no one seems to mind or notice.

It was last year that we were at a rooftop party at the Met, honoring some artist or charity, it's hard to keep track. It was your standard cocktail soiree—white tent, passed appetizers, a jazz quartet, and a magnificent view of Central Park and the lights of the city. I wore a velvet dress that had been my mother's.

I stood next to my dad, while he spoke with people I didn't recognize, but who seemed to know him well. I glanced around the scene, and caught Amos's eye on the other end of the party. He appeared to be stuck in the same situation with Louisa. He half-smiled at me, and tilted his head toward the exit. I slipped away from my dad unnoticed, and wove through the crowds. I got to the doors, where I found Amos, waiting for me.

"Tuna tartare or mini moo shu?" he asked as he offered me the appetizers.

"Moo shu," I replied.

We went back down to the museum, which had stayed open for the guests to enjoy that evening. It was eerie and beautiful to walk around the massive Great Hall, which ordinarily is filled to the brim with tourists, but that night was empty except for Amos and me. Our footsteps echoed as we wordlessly headed through Egyptian Art, quickly passing the tombs and mummies.

We arrived at the Temple of Dendur, and just held our breath for a moment. It felt like stepping into another realm. It was magical to be in the space at night and all alone. We walked up the steps to the main platform. It felt ethereal, as if we were floating above the reflective pool that surrounded the structure. We sat down on the ledge, and gazed at the ancient relic and giant sphinx sculptures.

"Holy shit, it's beautiful here," Amos said.

"It's my favorite in the whole museum."

"Me too," Amos replied. And we just took in the space for a while. But then Amos turned to me. "So, are you going to the Gold and Silver Ball?" he asked, referring to the black-tie charity event that happens every winter. The party had basically become our private school prom—one of the most important events of the year.

"I don't think so . . ." My voice trailed off.

"Why not?"

"Well, you kind of have to be asked," I replied. "And that hasn't exactly happened."

"It will."

"I don't know. All of my friends are already fielding offers."

"Flynn, you're better than those girls."

"Aisha's been asked by three different guys."

"Seriously. You're smart, and cool . . . and pretty."

Suddenly I felt strange. Amos had never complimented me like that before. "You don't have to say that," I said with a shrug.

"I wouldn't say it if it wasn't true." I felt my cheeks instantly flush. "I'll go with you," he offered.

It caught me off guard. I laughed awkwardly. "That's pretty lame if I have to take my brother," I replied.

"But I'm not really your brother," Amos said, looking straight at me. We were the only two living breathing things in the enormous space, but somehow I felt like there wasn't enough air.

"What are you, then?" I asked.

At that moment, a security guard walked in, his boots clanking on the marble floor. I turned away from Amos. "We should probably get back to the party," I said, and stood up.

"Yeah." Amos got up, too.

I can't help but wonder now what would have happened if Amos had answered the question back then. We ended up going to the dance with a big group, but I never forgot that offer.

"Flynn!" I turn to hear Neel yelling, as he stands through his sunroof, waving us down.

"Come on, guys!" I call out to Poppy and Amos, and we run back to Neel's car.

AMOS

I can't believe Neel pulled that do-you-know-who-my-father-is bullshit back at the hotel pool—and that it worked. I also can't believe Flynn even suggested I call Clay earlier. Yeah, right. There is no way I'm calling him. Not like it would be weird to see him. At least, I don't think it would be. I guess I'd have to make up some excuse about our whole running-away situation, but Clay is so clueless, I bet he wouldn't even ask.

It's not like I'd call him right now anyway. Because we're currently standing in a massive line outside some sneaker store on La Brea. Neel assured Poppy that the stop was on the way to the Hollywood sign, and that we'd still get there in time for the sunset. But now we've been waiting for twenty minutes, and I can tell Poppy is getting nervous that this is taking too long. Flynn and Neel snake their way to the front to find Neel's friend, while Poppy and I hang back.

The dude next to us obsessively checks his Twitter feed,

trying to figure out the location of some taco truck, while his friend worries they won't have his shoe size by the time they make it inside. Sometimes life can really feel like a spoof, and I'm embarrassed to even be here. Finally, Flynn and Neel appear with some other kid—he's tall and lanky with a mop of curly brown hair. He's all, "You must be the runaways!" and fist-bumps me. He introduces himself as David Shapiro. He opens a shoe box, showing off his limited-edition Nikes. "Dope, right?" he asks, assuming we'd be impressed. I don't respond. "Man, my parents would kill me if I pulled a stunt like you guys. It'd be like, peace out, world, David has left the building. Like, RIP, me," he continues.

Who is this guy? I say to myself as we walk back to Neel's double-parked car and get in.

"Shappy's parents are psychiatrists," Neel explains.

"Which means I'm majorly maladjusted," Shappy adds. "But seriously, you guys just bounced from the airport?"

"It all happened kind of quickly, but yeah." Flynn shrugs.

"Things with your parents must be pretty dark."

"Something like that," she says.

Poppy shivers, and rests her head on my shoulder. She must be cold from swimming, and tired from the long day, but she doesn't complain. Even though she has an old soul, sometimes I'm struck by how young she really is. I can't believe Jack and Louisa are doing this to her. No kid is ever prepared for the catastrophe of divorce. It changes you. Because it makes you realize that everything's impermanent, nothing is sacred, and you're all alone in this world.

Things get complicated when you try to fill the void. That's what got so messed up last year. Flynn and I were hanging out all the time, and it all just started to feel too confusing. I told her more than I've ever told any of those overpriced Manhattan therapists Louisa has sent me to over the years. Like about the time when I was six and I found Clay bloody and sprawled out on the kitchen floor, and I thought he was dead, so I called 911. Of course, he wasn't dead, just blitzed out of his mind. Later that day, Clay sat at the foot of my bed and cried, promising me he'd never drink again. Back then I was young enough to believe him.

Clay has reached out a bunch over the past year, claiming to be clean now, wanting to "talk," but I don't buy it, and I don't call him back. You can only be played for a fool so many times. More than anything, I just wish he'd stop calling. He sent me some bullshit texts last year, right before a big lacrosse game. He said he was thinking about the time he let me ditch the first-grade spelling bee so I could drive with him upstate to look at the fall foliage. Clay always liked to reminisce when he was drunk or stoned. Why does he get to hold on to the good memories while I'm stuck with all the others?

Needless to say, the lacrosse game was a disaster. I couldn't get those stupid texts out of my head. I got kicked out in the first half for a personal foul, and I gave the ref a piece of my mind. When I got home that night, it was like I was pulled by some greater force (genetics, perhaps) straight to the liquor cabinet. I grabbed a bottle of Grey Goose and slammed the door to my room. I hated how it tasted, and I hated how it made me feel. But I did it anyway. Hours later, there was a knock on my door. I didn't answer, but Flynn still came in. She sat down next to me on the floor and gently pulled the bottle away from me. I put my head down and hugged my knees into my chest. Flynn rested her head gently on my shoulder, and it took everything in me not to break down and cry. I knew I could cry in front of Flynn, but I didn't want to. Clay didn't deserve my tears.

"You're not him," she said.

I lifted my head up. "How do you know? You've never met him."

"Because I know," Flynn said. And even though deep down I knew that she was right, I needed to hear it. I rubbed my forehead; my head had started to throb. The vodka swishing around in my empty stomach wasn't helping the situation, either.

"How you feeling?"

"Flammable."

"Well, I have some good news. Rosie's making chicken fajitas for dinner. I put in a request," she added.

"That's the best thing I've heard all day."

And with that, she stood up, reached her hand out, and pulled me up. "Let's eat."

I know that Flynn and I are sort of siblings, but she's never totally felt like a sister, and never totally felt like just a friend, either. I guess because she's unlike anyone I've ever known. I mean, yeah, she's beautiful. Maybe not in the obvious, blond-hair-big-boobs way that guys my age notice, but it's no secret that guys my age are total idiots. Her long limbs, which once looked gawky, now appear womanly.

I see the way this Neel kid is looking at her. He knows. He

knows she's special. That she's not like the other girls. That she's kind and innocent—and not in a way that seems silly or naïve. Maybe that's why I feel this need to protect her. But maybe that's the problem: It's too much pressure. Being there for her—for each other. Because if I have learned anything over the past few years, it's that I should never depend on anyone. And Flynn needed to learn that, too.

She turns around from the front seat and lays her scarf on Poppy's lap like a blanket. She smiles at me, and despite myself, I smile back. Poppy yawns, fighting to keep her eyes open.

"Are we there yet?" she whimpers.

The late-afternoon sun is just starting to set as we turn up Laurel Canyon. "We're almost there," I tell her.

POPPY

I can't believe I'm here. Up in the Hollywood Hills, looking at the Hollywood sign. I read in one of my books that the time just before sunset is called magic hour in moviemaking. It's my favorite time of day—because when you take a picture, it looks like the whole world is painted gold. It makes real life look, well, magical.

Someday, when I'm old and glamorous and I write my memoir, I will remember this as one of the most exciting times in my life. The title of the book will be *Runaway.* I've been called a lot of things in my short life—freak, loser, weirdo, the list goes on—but I never thought I'd be a runaway. A runaway sounds adventurous and intriguing—like Princess Ann in *Roman Holiday*! Definitely not someone you'd call a loser. And definitely not something I'm going to miss out on because I don't have my stupid pills.

I feel so far away—from New York, and Rosie, and Mom and Dad. Sure, my parents travel all the time without me, but

I've never traveled anywhere without them. It's pretty fun. It almost feels like this could be my new life. If we were to stay here in Los Angeles, I know that Flynn and Amos would take good care of me. They always do. It's just that Mom and Dad are always so busy with work and traveling that it's almost like they forget about me. Like on my ninth birthday.

I didn't even want to have a party, but Mom said that it would be good for me to invite all the girls from my class over to celebrate. I agreed, but only because I was going to have an Audrey Hepburn–themed party. Mom and Rosie begged me to pick something the other girls my age would be into. But it was my birthday, and I wanted an ode to Audrey. I would wear a black dress with white satin gloves just like Holly Golightly in *Breakfast at Tiffany's,* and we'd hang movie posters all over the apartment. We would eat crustless cucumber sandwiches and profiteroles from Sant Ambroeus on Madison. And then on Monday, everyone at school would talk about how I threw the best birthday party of the year, and I wouldn't have to eat lunch alone anymore.

Mom and Dad were out of town the week leading up to the party, but Rosie had everything covered. And Mom promised they would be back that morning, just in time. So I woke up on February 5, a little nervous but mostly excited about my party. I looked out my window and saw the city covered in snow. I've always loved the snow—maybe it's because I was born during a snowstorm. Mom said the traffic getting to the hospital was so bad, she was worried she was going to have to deliver me right in the taxi! Luckily for all of us, she didn't.

I hurried downstairs for breakfast and found Flynn, Amos, and Rosie waiting for me. They gave me birthday hugs, but I could tell something was wrong. The kitchen TV was on—the word BLIZZARD flashing across it. Uh-oh. Rosie said my mom had called to say that their flight was canceled, and that we'd just have to celebrate when they got back. I tried not to cry as I watched the weatherman tell everyone to stay inside.

"Don't worry—almost all of the girls live uptown. They'll come," Flynn said as she put her arm around me. But no one came. Not one. The party was supposed to start at noon, and at around eleven-thirty the calls started coming. I could hear Flynn in the other room talking to Tatiana's mom, and Kaylie's mom, and all the rest of them. She said that she understood, that yes, the weather outside was awful, and that yes, of course, if it stopped snowing, everyone should definitely still come over. I ran back to my room and got under the covers. Maybe if I closed my eyes and fell back asleep, I would wake up and find that this was all just a bad dream.

A few hours later, I woke up to the sound of Flynn playing "Moon River," the theme song from *Breakfast at Tiffany's,* on the piano. I went downstairs and found Flynn at the Steinway, and Amos next to her. They were all dressed up and waiting for me. Amos took my hands and danced with me around the living room, and even though I kept stepping on his feet, it didn't matter. Soon I forgot all about my stupid party.

After we delivered a slice of marble birthday cake to everyone who worked in the building, Flynn and Amos gave me my present. I carefully unwrapped the box and found a vintage Polaroid inside.

"We saw it at the Chelsea flea market and thought you'd like it," Flynn said as I inspected the camera.

"I more than like it. I love it!" They showed me how to load the special film they had to order online, and other than that, it's pretty easy to use. I couldn't have asked for a more perfect present, or more perfect siblings. Because when the three of us are together, it's like everything else that's going wrong in the world doesn't bother me.

Now, almost a year later, I use my birthday camera to take a picture of Flynn looking out over Los Angeles. Everything below looks so small, it's like nothing can touch us, and I wish there were a way to hold on to this feeling. I watch her eyeing Neel, who's goofing around with that Shappy guy. I definitely think she has a crush on him.

"Look over at me," I call to Flynn. She turns around and gives me a half smile, and I take another photo of her.

"C'mon, let's take one of the two of us," she says.

"Amos too," I add.

"It's getting late. We should get going," Amos grumbles. He's been waiting over by Neel's car.

"One picture. Please? We have to get the sunset!" Amos shakes his head but walks over anyway.

"Neel, do you mind taking our picture?" I ask. Neel grabs the camera from me. I put my arms around Flynn and Amos and squeeze them extra tight.

"Say . . . Hollywood!" Shappy calls out over Neel's shoulder. But even though none of us say it, I know we are all smiling. Even Amos. I know I shouldn't have told Flynn and Amos about the divorce, and I know this bubble won't last forever, but for right now, I just want to pretend that I'm living in a movie—where I'm the star, and there are only happy endings.

FLYNN

I wander down the aisle at a convenience store, grabbing three toothbrushes and a pack of Christmas-colored M&M's, which I'm sure Amos will make me put back. We stopped here on our way to Neel's house and all immediately dispersed in the store. My hair is knotty from swimming, so I grab a small leave-in conditioner, too. There are some girls next to me in tiny cutoffs and huge sweatshirts, inspecting shampoos and huddled in deep conversation.

"I can't believe you sent him that picture," the blonde says to the brunette.

"What's the big deal?" the brunette asks. "You sext all the time."

"Yeah—with my boyfriend." The brunette now looks petrified. "Whatever," the blonde continues. "At least people won't think you're a tease anymore. And you do have great tits." The brunette shrugs, and the girls head off. I hear them in the next aisle, running into Shappy. Somehow it doesn't surprise me that they know each other.

I continue down the aisle, and I can't help but blush a little when I pass the condoms. I make sure no one is nearby as I linger, curious to check out the options. Who knew there were so many choices? I guess non-virgins. I know I'm supposed to be mature, and it's not a big deal, but isn't it kind of a big deal that people just buy these things all the time? Twenty-four hours a day. In broad daylight. And I mean, who knows what could happen with Neel later? Isn't it better if I'm prepared?

I spot Amos rounding the corner, coming down the other end of the aisle. He looks at me, and then at the condoms. Busted, I quickly turn in the opposite direction.

"Hey, Flynn," Neel whispers from the corner of the store. I head over to him.

"Hey," I say.

"So, what's your ID situation?" he asks conspiratorially.

"I've just got my passport."

"Shit. And my fake got shredded in the dryer last week."

Shappy shuffles over, shaking his head. "The dude at the front does not look friendly."

"And I asked some old lady if she'd do a good deed and help us out, and she looked at me like I was a straight-up terrorist or something," Neel adds.

"Why can't we just drink what's at your dad's?" Shappy questions.

"I'm telling you, he pays people to notice shit like that," Neel says. "Beer we can steal from the garage. But if we want anything hard, we've got to get it ourselves." We stand there, stumped. The front door opens, and a bunch of rowdy college guys come plowing into the store.

"This is perfect. Flynn, it's all you," Shappy says.

"What's all me?" I ask, dreading the answer.

"You gotta ask those bro-tards to buy us some booze."

"I dunno . . . I'm, um, not really good at stuff like that," I stammer.

"But you're our last hope," Shappy pleads.

"He's kind of right," Neel says. "And there's no way those dudes are going to say no to a hot girl."

"Okay," I say. "I can try." Wait. Did Neel just say he thinks I'm hot?

"Here." Neel hands me a fifty. "They can keep the change." I nod, and take a deep breath. I walk over to two of the guys—they're in jeans and USC hoodies, and definitely not the cutest ones of the group. I feel bad about singling them out, but I figure they're my best bet. They're clearly watching me. *Be confident like Meredith,* I think as I saunter up to them. *Be flirty like Aisha. Be anyone but yourself right now.*

"Hey," I say, attempting to sound sexy and inviting.

"Hey there," the chubbier one of the two says. I attempt to play the part of a tourist just looking to party. The whole thing feels so forced and weird, I don't even recognize the sound of my own voice. But somehow, it works. Outside the store, the guys slip me a bottle of Cuervo, and I promise to call them later to meet up with the rest of my really hot and single friends. Their whole herd heads out, and I breathe a sigh of relief. Awkward mission accomplished.

31

AMOS

She scurried away like a little kid, her hand caught in the condom jar. She couldn't possibly be sleeping with Neel. Could she? I have to stop being so blind when it comes to Flynn. I pass the display and can't help but think about the afternoon last spring when I became a man, so to speak. I had been hooking up with this girl Claire Chandler for exactly three weeks. I knew she wasn't a virgin. Everybody did. She had a boyfriend in college, but they had broken up over spring break. I knew she was just trying to make him jealous, but I didn't care. It was a Tuesday afternoon, and she invited me to come over to watch a movie. I was just grateful that at least one of us would know what we were doing.

When I got home that night, Flynn was in the kitchen making mint tea. "Claire is really pretty," she said as she took another mug out of the cabinet. Man, word travels fast.

"Yeah," I answered, not really knowing what else to say. As

Flynn handed me my mug, I noticed that there was something off about her tonight. Something wounded. Jealous? Maybe she just felt weird that I hadn't told her about Claire. Flynn and I talked about everything, but we never really talked about girls. Sure, she knew the headlines, but I didn't think she needed to know the specifics. It wasn't like I was hiding anything. It was just that Flynn and I talked about real things—like our favorite books, and Bill Murray movies, and how we want to climb Machu Picchu one day. And it wasn't like there was much to hide anyway. Lately, I'd found that the more time I spent with Flynn, the harder it got for me to hang out with other girls who were just pretty, or just fun, or just down to hook up. Compared to Flynn, all the other girls just felt so . . . fleeting.

And it wasn't like Claire was about to become my girlfriend. She texted me after finals were over, saying that she was having people out to her family's house on Fire Island to celebrate the end of our sophomore year. While the offer was tempting, I didn't really want to go. Flynn and I had just started watching *Mad Men,* and we had big post-finals plans to binge on sushi and TV. And so I texted Claire back that I was going to lie low in the city. I knew that would be the end of Claire Chandler and me, but I didn't care.

With most of our friends off to their country homes or summer camps or Europe, Jack on one of his business trips, and Louisa already out in Amagansett with Poppy, Flynn and I were left to fend for ourselves. Flynn didn't leave for camp for another week, and my only plan for the summer was to train for lacrosse, bum around the Hamptons, and study for the SATs. For that one week, it felt like Flynn and I were the only people on the entire island of Manhattan, which was a good thing, considering we had a million hours of *Mad Men* to get through.

Holy shit, that show is good. We were glued to the TV for hours on end—day turned into night. Season 1 turned into season 4. It was like Flynn and I were living in suspended time. We snacked on grilled cheese and martinis that we made for ourselves from the vodka we had delivered courtesy of Jack's Sherry-Lehmann house charge. And when we needed to stretch our legs, we'd take a walk down Madison Avenue and imagine what New York was like back in the swinging sixties.

The night before she left, we decided to go to PJ Clarke's for dinner, since they go there on the show. After we'd finished our burgers and Flynn had fed the jukebox all our change, we headed out. But as we stepped onto Third Avenue, there was a roll of thunder, and suddenly the sky opened up.

It was rush hour—we didn't stand a chance of getting a cab. We had no choice but to make a run for it. I took her hand, and we ran as fast as we could, getting more and more drenched with each block. We finally got back home, and as we fell into our apartment, we took one look at each other—soaked to the bone—and burst into laughter. It was a good thing Louisa was gone, because she would have lost her shit seeing the mess we were making in the foyer. I raced to the linen closet and grabbed a towel to wrap around Flynn. I rubbed her arms, trying to dry her off. She looked up at me and smiled.

"Thanks," she said as she used the towel to wring out her

hair. I couldn't help but notice that her white T-shirt had become see-through, revealing the flower pattern on her bra and the outline of her small breasts. I quickly looked away. We went off to our respective rooms. I knew she was stressed about last-minute packing, so I tried to stay out of her way for the rest of the night. I could hear her on the phone, saying goodbye to her friends, promising to keep in touch, the things that only girls do. It hit me that I'd be without her for the rest of the summer—and that I'd miss her.

Just before midnight, I went to her room. She was in boxers and an oversized Spence T-shirt, zipping up her suitcase.

"Think we can plow through the final episodes before you go?" I asked.

"I guess I can sleep on the plane. We can watch here," she said, queuing up the next episode on her laptop. I lay down next to her. In all the time Flynn and I had spent together, we had never been like this. Together, on a bed. *She's your sister,* I said to myself. Why did I suddenly need a reminder? I hit play, and the episode started.

The next thing I knew it was the middle of the night, Flynn's room lit by the glow of the computer screen. It took me a second to realize that we had fallen asleep together. I watched her shoulders move up and down with her breath. I watched her lips, open ever so slightly. I knew I could slip out and go back to my room, but I didn't want to. Instead, I moved closer. She stirred, and when she opened her eyes and saw me, she froze.

"Hi," she said tentatively.

"Hi." My hesitation matched hers.

Her hair fell onto her face, and without thinking, I tucked it behind her ear. A gesture so simple, but it felt like more. As we looked at each other through the darkness, we both knew that we were headed into uncharted territory. I needed her closer. I needed . . . her. And so I kissed her. I don't know if we kissed for a second or a minute or an hour. I've replayed it so many times in my head, and it's different every time.

The next thing I remember is waking up to the sound of the elevator doors opening, and our housekeeper, Thelma, humming as she came inside. I shot up, my eyes squinting from the sun blaring into Flynn's room. I looked over at her bedside clock, which read 7:58 a.m. Her flight was at seven. She was gone. I quietly got out of bed—I didn't want Thelma to see me in here. I crept back to my room and found a note on my desk. *xo, Flynn* was all it said. I picked up my phone and started to text her. But I didn't have the faintest idea what to say.

I went out to get some breakfast, even though I wasn't hungry. I sat at the counter at EJ's and picked at my scrambled eggs until my coffee got cold. My phone buzzed in my pocket, and I jumped. But it was just Louisa, asking when she could expect me in the Hamptons. I didn't write back. I clicked over to Flynn's name and tried to write something to her. But every time I started to type, my mind would just go blank. I put my phone back in my pocket.

I spent the rest of the day cleaning out all my papers and notes from the school year—it felt good to just get rid of all of it. So long, Algebra II—I hope to never see you again. And when I came across one of the many catalogs for Phillips Academy Andover that Louisa had periodically placed in my room, I gave it a second look. I had spent the past year weighing the pros and cons of going away to boarding school for my junior and senior years. Of course, it was all Louisa had ever wanted for me, but the idea of following in my dad's footsteps (and those of all the Abernathys who came before me) wasn't exactly appealing. Suddenly, escaping didn't seem like the worst idea.

I took my phone out again—the blinking cursor of the blank text to Flynn taunting me. Still I had no idea what to say. So instead I called Louisa. I told her that I would be in the Hamptons later that day, and that she should tell the dean at Andover to expect me there in the fall.

32

FLYNN

"Shotgun!" Poppy shouts as we all gleefully run through the convenience store parking lot, hoping no one saw our booze deal go down.

"Oh shit!" Shappy yells, and races her to Neel's car. But Poppy gets there first, and I have to say I'm proud. She takes her rightful position up front, while I crawl into the middle seat next to Amos. Shappy gets in after me, squishing me closer to Amos. Our legs touch.

"Sorry," I say, as I shift my body away from his.

"Don't worry about it," he replies. *Don't worry about it? Okay, Amos.* Considering I already have a growing list of things that I worry about in regard to Amos, I suppose it's nice not to have to add another. Sometimes I wonder if that night ever even happened. The only reason I know that it did, and that it isn't just a bizarre figment of my twisted imagination, is that I can't think of any other reason why Amos and I are sitting here so close to each other, yet feel so far apart.

I had been thinking that whole June night about how much I was going to miss him while I was away. I had spent the past few hours on the phone telling Sabrina and Aisha how much I would miss them—even though I really wouldn't. And yet I couldn't just walk down the hall and say the same thing to Amos—even though I really would. I just felt like it would be weird. Or what if he thought I was weird for saying something like that? And why had I been stalking Claire Chandler online ever since they hooked up? Amos had always hooked up with lots of girls. It had never really bothered me before. Up until that night, I'd never thought anything like that would ever happen between Amos and me. But then it did happen. After we kissed, he looked at me in a way I had never been looked at before. We didn't talk; we just kept kissing. And then he held me, my head on his chest. Eventually he fell asleep, but I didn't. I needed to stay awake to know that I hadn't dreamed it.

In the car on the way to the airport that morning, I couldn't stop checking my phone. I was sure Amos would text or something. I checked it again once I got through security. Then at the gate. And then when we boarded. A lump was forming in my throat. Maybe he regretted what happened? Or maybe I was just like his other inconsequential girls?

Now here we are, six months and three thousand miles from that night, and I still have the same lump in my throat. The same unanswered questions between us. Neel's car speeds through a dark tunnel. And when we emerge, it's like we're in a totally different world. The freeway has ended, and the Pacific Ocean is immediately to our left. I glance over at Amos, his gaze fixed out the window, and I wonder if anything will ever be normal with us again.

33

AMOS

By the time we get to Malibu, it's dark out. Neel pulls over onto a small driveway right off the highway, and we all pile out of the car. He enters a code into a keypad and lets us pass, one by one. Once we're through the gate, we can see straight into the glass fortress and out the other side, where the moon glistens on the glassy Pacific. Okay, so he wasn't fronting—Neel's obviously loaded. We're instructed to take our shoes off and leave them in the basket by the front door.

"It's an Indian thing," he tells us as we walk inside.

"Whoa, is that the ocean?" Poppy asks. The lure of the water pulls Poppy and Flynn through the house and out onto the back terrace. Neel watches Flynn with a self-satisfied smirk that makes me want to hurl.

The house itself looks like a spaceship. It's super modern with all white walls and high ceilings. There's art everywhere. I recognize some of the pieces—it's not like I'm some aficionado, but I've picked up a few things over the years from my mom. I can hear Louisa's voice in my head saying that the Khans' taste is nouveau. That they're not real collectors. I'd have to agree.

"Make yourselves at home. *Mi casa es su casa,*" Neel tells us. Really, bro? Be more of a cliché. How many times has he dangled this view before some unsuspecting girl?

Be careful, Flynn, I try to telepath to her. But it's like the signal has been lost on the wireless connection that used to exist between us—the one that let us catch each other's eye, across the dinner table or at a party, and with one glance know exactly what the other one was thinking.

Instead she just looks at Neel and shyly asks, "You're sure your dad won't mind if we crash here?"

"He and my stepmom are out of the country on set, and won't be back until the new year."

"So you got Home Alone-d for the holidays . . . that's a move we're familiar with," I remark.

"Yeah, well, Diwali was a while back. We don't really do the Christmas thing, although I do love me some latkes."

A short Latina woman in all white emerges from a room off the kitchen. Neel introduces us to his housekeeper, Bebe, and judging by his reverential tone, you can tell she runs the ship around here. Makes me miss Rosie. I wonder what will happen to her in the divorce. Bebe eyes each of us, and I know she can sense that Flynn, Poppy, and I are up to something, but she's not quite sure what. In the meantime, she thankfully takes pity on us, and leads Poppy and Flynn upstairs to find a change of clothes.

FLYNN

The scissors crunch through one last chunk, and I watch a thick lock of hair float down—the strands scattering everywhere as soon as they hit the marble bathroom floor. I stare at myself in the mirror above the sink, and grin. The cut is shorter than I planned—it falls just below my chin—but once I had the scissors in my hands, it felt so good, I couldn't stop. The more I cut, the more I wanted to shed the old me. My fingers graze the back of my neck—exposed to air for the first time since I was a little girl with a neat little bob. The ends are ragged and not totally even, but it's not awful for a first attempt at DIY hairstyling. It's kind of messy, and I like it. I stand there for a minute, in my underwear, and look at myself in the full-length mirror. I haven't noticed until now, but my legs look stronger from all my running. It makes me proud. Like maybe change is possible.

"Whoa!" Neel exclaims from the doorway. I quickly reach

for a towel and wrap it around my half-naked body. My eyes fall to the mess of hair covering the floor.

"Sorry. I'll clean everything up."

"It's all good," Neel says, and I can't even imagine what he must be thinking about me right now.

"So, pizza or Thai?" he asks.

"What?"

"For dinner."

"Dinner . . . amazing. I'm starving."

"It all comes down to you, Barlow. We've got two votes for pizza from the East Coast, and two for Thai from the West Coast."

"Hmmm, that's a true dilemma. While I have allegiances to both, I think I'm going to have to side with my siblings on this one."

"Fair enough."

"Can you get a separate small pizza for Poppy? Mushrooms and olives. No cheese. And gluten-free crust."

"Are you sure she's not from LA?" he says with a grin that always makes me blush. "Come down whenever you're ready." Neel walks out, but then pops his head back in.

"Hey, Flynn?"

"Yeah?"

"You look hot . . . with your hair like that."

POPPY

"Ven aquí, pobrecita," Bebe says to me as she leads me into Neel's little sister's room. It's hard to tell how old the girl is. I know it's rude to snoop, but I can't help it. My mom would say I'm being nosy, but I like to think of myself as curious. Trouble is, there isn't much to find. Just by looking around, you can tell her parents are divorced. I've known enough daughters of divorce in New York City to know how to recognize it. Like someone lives here, but not really. The drawers are half-empty; there are no notepads with doodles, no yearbooks, no candy wrappers stashed under the bed. Like it's a room for a pretend daughter the parent wishes existed, or maybe a little girl who used to exist but doesn't anymore. Or maybe she does, but only every other weekend.

I wonder if I'm going to become that phantom girl. With that empty room. I guess Mom will take me most of the time, just because she's the mom and that's what happens. But maybe I'd fit in better somewhere else. Maybe if I move to the Bay Area with Dad and Flynn, I'll be happier. Maybe I'll have friends. Maybe they won't think I'm strange. If Flynn's from there, it must be okay.

But what if Dad doesn't want me to go with them? Or what if I go all the way there, and the kids don't like me at my new school, either? Maybe I don't belong anywhere. Maybe I should just go to school online, and then I won't have to worry about bothering anyone anymore.

Normally, when I start to feel this way, I tell Rosie, and she hugs me real tight and says, "There, there, love." She tells me to take three deep breaths, and if I'm still not feeling good after that, she gives me a little pill, and it's like everything starts moving a little slower. But Rosie isn't here, and I'm too scared to tell Flynn and Amos about my Bora Bora–bound pills. I don't want them to think I need to go home—that I'm not grown-up like them. That I'm not . . . normal. I've always wondered what would happen if I stopped taking my medicine. I guess now I'll finally find out.

AMOS

I help myself to a look around the place while Poppy and Flynn disappear upstairs. Shappy makes himself at home. He plops down on the couch and puts his dirty feet up on the perfectly white sofa. I laugh to myself, thinking how Louisa would have this kid ejected if he ever tried that in our house. That's one thing that's nice about being away at boarding school—I don't have to worry anymore about the land mines that make up my mother's anal-retentiveness. I think she's getting worse as she gets older. And as Jack gets richer. Something happens to rich people. It's like they're on some warped power trip—where they think they can control every single part of their existence and the world around them.

"Check it out," Shappy says as he pushes a button, and out of nowhere a screen slides down from the ceiling.

"Dope," I say somewhat sarcastically—though any nuance of tone is lost on him.

"Wait till you see the screening room," he adds. This is exactly what's wrong with LA. When Flynn, Poppy, and I took off on this adventure, I thought we were heading for something bigger—something that meant something. This was supposed to be about us. But now I'm looking around this garish house and wondering what in the world we are doing here.

"Actually, is there a computer I could use?" I ask. Shappy lifts his chin in the direction of an adjacent study.

I settle into the office chair, power up the iMac on the desk, and even though I'm not totally sure if I should, sign into my email account. Louisa and Jack may not be good parents—hell, they may not even be good people—but I'm not sure they deserve what we're probably putting them through.

And there it is. Sixty-five new messages staring back at me on the screen. Most of them frantic emails in the last hour from Jack and Louisa. This means it's true. The piece I've tried to push out of my head. Despite my efforts to ignore the time, it's now undeniable. Our plane has landed in Bora Bora. And we're not on it. All the passengers have disembarked. Well, all save three. By now, Jack and Louisa are berating some poor slob at the airline and anyone else they can accost, and have most likely gathered that we arrived safely in Los Angeles, according to our itinerary, and then never boarded our connecting flight.

I quickly scan through the messages, which start out inquisitive and then run the gamut to downright irate. I naïvely hoped that they would trust that we haven't been kidnapped, raped, and sold into child slavery and instead assume that we are simply acting like the spoiled, entitled, disappointing children they thought us to be.

But they sound angry and alarmed in a way I've never heard, and suddenly I'm realizing that we're in way deeper than we ever planned. I see the words *MISSING CHILD REPORT* and *POLICE.* I hear Flynn come down the steps, and I quickly close the browser window and clear the history. I don't know what tonight or tomorrow has in store for us, but I know one thing for sure—we are running on borrowed time.

37

FLYNN

"Aren't you going to say anything?" I ask Amos, as he looks at me, not even flinching at the sight of my short hair. He stands in the kitchen, where Poppy and I sit at the enormous island, snacking on tortilla chips and guacamole that Bebe made for us.

"They're freaking out," he says.

"What do you mean?" I nearly choke on a chip. "You *talked* to them?"

"I just checked my email. And it's not good. They're calling the police."

"Oh shit!" Shappy calls out from the other room.

"They're worried something actually happened to us," Amos continues. "You guys see how messed up this is, right?"

"I know we should feel bad that we're ruining Mom and Dad's vacation, but they're about to ruin our lives. I really don't want to leave," Poppy chimes in.

"Well, what if we just tell them that?" I suggest.

Amos rolls his eyes at me.

"I'm serious. Let's tell them we know about the divorce and we're not coming on the trip. We can assure them that we're alive and well, but we just need some time. And we'll be back in touch when we're ready," I propose.

"Oh yeah, I'm sure they'll go for that," Amos sarcastically quips.

"Please," Poppy begs. "I'll never ask you for anything again. I just want more time with us together. Can we please just stay here a little longer?"

"Come on, Amos. We have to show them that no matter what, we refuse to be separated."

He bites his lip, skeptical. "What do you mean? Like an ultimatum?"

"Exactly!" I exclaim. "Don't you want to take a stand against the tyranny of divorce?" I continue, my voice getting stronger. This is more than just a silly act of rebellion, and I can see Amos knows that.

He considers our plea. "We can give it a shot . . . but don't blame me when the US marshal comes a-calling." Amos thinks for a second. "Shappy, lemme borrow your phone." Shappy gets up from the couch and tosses his phone to Amos. "Here goes nothing." Amos takes a deep breath and types: "Dear Jack and Louisa, we are together, and we are safe."

"And we're not coming back!" Poppy pipes in.

"Let me work on the language." Amos continues to type as Neel waltzes into the kitchen with the pizza.

"Who's hungry?" Neel asks.

Poppy and I sit down at the table and dig in. "Well, I sent it," Amos says as he hands the phone back to Shappy. I take a bite of warm tomatoey cheesy goodness, and relax a little—it seems like we'll get to stay on this adventure . . . at least for a little bit longer.

After dinner, Shappy breaks out the bottle of Cuervo and suggests he and Neel call some girls over. And I swear, Neel looks at me when he says that he's "all good." Shappy then turns to Amos, who corroborates by saying, "Not tonight." Not surprisingly, shortly thereafter Shappy says he has to bounce, and he calls an Uber. So Poppy, Amos, Neel, and I hit up the screening room while Bebe retreats to her bedroom off the kitchen.

Poppy is wired from what's turning into the longest day ever, so we all agree to let her pick the movie, which means we're watching another one of her favorites, *Edward Scissorhands*. I'm trying to focus on the screen, but it's hard with Neel's hand on my inner thigh, under one of what seems like an infinite supply of Neel's father's cashmere blankets. I'm pretending not to be fixated on his hand slowly inching up my leg, even though it's literally the only thing I can think about. His hand. On my leg. Neel, however, seems entirely relaxed—like we live in a world where hands and legs are always meant to be touching. Who knows, maybe they are.

An hour and a half later, Poppy is fast asleep, curled up in a blanket at the end of the row that Neel and I are in. Amos sits alone, in the front row. On the screen, Winona and Johnny are dancing in the fake snow, which means the movie's almost over. Then we'll all have to go our separate ways to bed, and

I'm already getting anxious about what's going to happen. What do I want to happen?

I hate feeling like this. I hate feeling so . . . unsure. But that's not really true. I know what I want. At least I think I do. I guess if I'm being totally honest, I hate knowing what I want and not knowing if I'm going to get it.

Like when Aisha's dad gave her two tickets to Beyoncé a few weeks ago. And I knew I wanted to go. But I also knew Sabrina wanted to go. And I also knew Sabrina well enough to know that she always gets what she wants. In other words, no matter how she engineered for us to "fairly" decide who got the ticket, the end result would be her backstage at Beyoncé and me back at home. So I told Sabrina to take the ticket. That I was over Beyoncé anyway.

But I'm sick of taking the backseat, of just letting life happen—to other people. I'm sick of giving away what I want. So when the movie's done, and Amos takes Poppy upstairs to Neel's sister's room, I grab Neel's hand and lead him into his bedroom.

38

AMOS

It's the middle of the night, and I'm awake. I tell myself to go back to sleep, but my mind is racing. I can't lie here any longer, so I get up and tiptoe downstairs. There's something simultaneously unnerving and comforting about being the only person awake in a house full of people sleeping. I go into the kitchen and start to pour myself a glass of water from the tap, but suddenly I'm thirsty for something else.

The bar is set up in the living room, and there's every kind of liquor on display. Top shelf. Not like I would expect anything less from Mr. Khan at this point. I realize I haven't had a real drink in almost four months. Sure, I'll sneak the occasional beer in my room at school, but seeing the way all the kids are so preoccupied with getting shit-faced makes it feel like pretty much the last thing I want to be doing. Having an alcoholic father really has a way of souring you on the stuff. But right now, I need something to take the edge off.

Neel seemed surprisingly concerned about protecting his dad's booze, but Shappy left with that bottle of shitty tequila. So, sorry, Neel. Looks like you're going to have to take one for the team here. I consider the bottle of Tanqueray, but there's only a little left. And anyway, my dad always said gin makes you angry. So I settle on scotch. Scotch feels like a drink meant for the middle of the night, and there's a big bottle of Macallan 18 with my name on it. As I take one of the crystal glasses neatly lined up on the shelf, my fingers slip, and I almost drop it. I need this drink more than I thought.

I pour a splash of amber liquid into the glass. I force it down in one gulp, feeling the burn of every drop, and promptly pour a little more. Drink in hand, I walk over to the sliding door that leads out onto the terrace, and I step outside.

There's a full moon tonight—it's hanging big and bright over the Pacific, and it looks, well, beautiful. The air is cool and damp, and I think about going inside to get a sweatshirt but take a warming sip of my drink instead. I forgot how cold LA gets at night, but then again, it's been a while since I've been here. I sit back on a lounge chair, and for a minute I just listen to the thunderous sound of the waves crashing.

I want to get lost in the rhythm of the water, but no matter how hard I try, my mind keeps going back to the same thing. The click of the lock on Neel's door, the sound of their hushed whispers. But if Flynn likes that douchebag, then she should do whatever she wants with him. It's not like I have any say in the mistakes she makes.

I know I was a total dick to her today. And that makes me feel like crap. Because that's the last thing I planned on. In some bizarre way, I was actually kind of looking forward to being on the boat. Even if our family is messed up, we're all we've got. And I thought that maybe it'd finally be time for us to talk about what happened back in June. But what's the point? Now that we're not going to be a family anymore, does that mean Flynn and I will just be . . . friends? Ex-stepsiblings? People who once knew each other?

"Of all the gin joints . . ."

I turn around, startled. There she is. She's wrapped in a blanket, and there's moonlight in her stupid short hair, and I can't really look at her because the second she appears, my heart starts beating faster. She takes a seat in the chair next to mine. We don't say anything for a minute. She looks at the glass of scotch on the ground in between us, reaches down, and takes a sip. She winces from the taste. She's still Flynn—whether she likes it or not. She puts the glass back down and then says, "I couldn't sleep, either."

We sit like this, in silence. And then, finally, I ask, "So, what made you do it?"

"Do what?"

"Run."

Flynn looks out at the ocean, and then just sort of shrugs. "Believe it or not, it seemed like the only reasonable option at the time." She thinks for a moment. "I can't face them. I can't think about what's going to happen next."

"At least you'll be going back home. Isn't that what you've always wanted?" I ask, hoping it's not true.

"I guess," she replies. And I can't help but wonder if it's really how she feels, or if she's just saying it to hurt me.

"Are you surprised? About the divorce?" I ask her.

She nods. "Which I'm sure you think is so naïve."

I do. But in a good way. "I hate to say it . . . but do you think it was Hans?" I ask her.

"Hans Gleitman? Really?"

"You saw how Louisa was always throwing herself at him whenever he was over for dinner. Calling him a visionary and whatnot. Saying his work was *transcendent,*" I say, mimicking my mom's air of pretension. Flynn cracks a smile. My Louisa impression is spot-on.

"Let's not jump to any conclusions," she says. Flynn always wants to see the best in people. "But his studio is in Amagansett. . . ." She trails off.

"I'm telling you. She has a type." Flynn looks distraught; her brow furrows. "What is it?" I ask.

"All this time, I wanted to think that my parents' divorce was okay because at least my dad had found what he was looking for in Louisa. Like it was worth it. But now that their marriage is over, too . . . I don't know what to think."

She picks some lint off her borrowed sweatpants.

"Just because something doesn't last, or doesn't turn out the way you thought it would, doesn't mean it wasn't worth it." I want her to believe me, but I don't think she does.

"It's just so . . . sad. All of it. Things ending. People leaving." She looks at me, and it's clear we're talking about more than Jack and Louisa.

"Flynn, I . . ." But I stop myself. There's so much I want to tell her. Like how sorry I am for leaving New York, for leaving her, without even a goodbye. And how I've spent the past few months trying to figure out what it is that I feel for her, but all this time later, I still don't know. And how sitting here now makes me glad we ran. I want to tell her all of this, but a strong wind blows, and she shivers from the cold. And suddenly I'm afraid of what I might say. Or do. So instead I say, "Come on. It's freezing. Let's go back inside."

We quietly slink back through the house. I follow Flynn upstairs, relieved when she slips into Poppy's room instead of Neel's.

39

FLYNN

My legs are burning, and I'm almost out of breath, so I turn around and head back to the house. I've probably only gone a mile or two, but running barefoot on the beach is harder than I anticipated. I woke up early—everyone else in the house was still deep in sleep, but I was weirdly wide awake. Blame it on the time change. But it was like the muscles in my body were begging me to move.

So here I am, in Neel's stepmother's coordinated Lululemon sports bra, tank top, and shorts, with the dog walkers and personal trainers on the beach in Malibu. The fog is so thick, it feels like I'm running through the clouds. Usually running helps clear my head, but today it's having the opposite effect. Because with every step, I'm flooded with memories of last night.

The door closed to Neel's room, and he pulled me in and kissed me. I had waited all summer to be with him, and now it was finally happening. We kissed for a while like that, standing up, until Neel led me over to the bed. Then we kissed lying down, which was nice, too. But the thing was, I couldn't get out of my head. I tried, I really did. But every time he put his hand somewhere, I'd think, *This is Neel's hand going up my shirt. This is Neel's hand going . . . other places.* I pulled away to catch my breath.

"You okay?" he asked me.

"Yeah," I answered.

"Okay," he said as he lifted my shirt up over my head. It all felt like it was moving so fast. My heart, his hands, everything. Could he tell I was a virgin? Was my virgin-ness something that non-virgins could detect?

"Neel . . . I'm a . . . you know, I've never . . . ," I said nervously.

"It's cool," he said. "Do you . . . want to?" he asked, in between kissing my neck.

"I . . . I don't know," I answered. "Maybe. But just . . . not, like, right now."

"That's okay. You're pretty fun to make out with," he said.

I could feel my cheeks turning red, but luckily, he couldn't see that in the dark. I woke up in the middle of the night with Neel snoring next to me. I got up to use the bathroom, and as I stood by the window looking out at the full moon, I noticed a silhouette on a lounge chair on the deck downstairs. I glanced back at Neel, still snoring, and tiptoed out.

There's still so much we need to talk about. Like how the last time I saw Amos, we were lying together in my bed. But I'm not ready to go there. Not yet. Last night was the first time in a long time that it felt like Amos and I were just hanging out like normal people. Normal people who had just happened to run away from their family vacation.

When Amos and I went inside, I didn't want to go back to Neel's room. Maybe it was because I didn't want Amos to see me go in there. Or maybe it was because I was worried it would be awkward waking up next to Neel. Or maybe it was because of his snoring. Either way, I crept into Neel's sister's room and crawled into bed with Poppy instead.

By the time I'm at the house, the fog has finally lifted, and it looks like an entirely different day. The sun is out, and there isn't a single cloud in the sky. I'm sweaty and panting as I slide open the glass door, and before I even have a minute to catch my breath, Poppy grabs my hand and drags me into the kitchen to proudly show me the breakfast feast she and Bebe have prepared.

"Welcome to Hotel Malibu!" Poppy says as she sits me down at the table, offering me coffee and orange juice. "Fresh squeezed—no pulp." She fills my glass with a smile because she knows that's just how I like it. Amos sits across from me, with a plate of chocolate chip pancakes piled high.

"Hope you're hungry," he says.

"Starving." I smile, relieved that we're at least starting the day off speaking. Poppy presents me with my own stack of pancakes, and then pours way too much maple syrup. I'm starving from my run, and I'm about to take my first bite when Neel walks in. All I can think about is that this person saw me half-naked a few hours ago. Should I say something, or should he? I should. No . . . he should.

"Hi," he says, looking right at me.

"Hey," I say.

"Well, what do you three gangstas have lined up for today?"

40

POPPY

I really wanted to go to Disneyland, but Neel said we couldn't because then we wouldn't be back in time to go to some party later. I could feel my cheeks turning red and my eyes filling up with tears, but Flynn just squeezed my hand and whispered in my ear that we were going to have the best day no matter where we were. She promised. I could tell she didn't want me to start crying in front of Neel. She gave me the same look my mom gives me when I'm about to have one of my "episodes," as she calls them. This will be the first full day I haven't taken my medicine, and I should maybe say something to Flynn or Amos about it, but I don't want them to worry. Or worse, I don't want them to call Mom and Dad.

So now we're wandering around Venice Beach, and while it's nothing like Disneyland, it's not like anywhere I've ever been. It kind of seems like a circus, but everyone is walking around like it's totally normal. There are people zipping by on bikes and skates, and even a guy on stilts. There are street performers, and a million stores selling T-shirts and jewelry I know Mom would call "trashy." I got excited when I saw a giant Ferris wheel over on a pier, and asked if we could go for a ride, but Neel and Flynn shot me down again. I don't really like Venice Beach at all. Flynn and Neel keep laughing at jokes that Amos and I don't seem to get. And then out of nowhere, Amos says he's got somewhere he needs to be.

"But we're all here. Where could you have to go?" I ask him. He says he has something to take care of, and he looks at Flynn. She's confused for a second, and then she just sort of nods. I forgot how they do this sometimes—speak to each other without using any words.

"Promise you'll come back?" I ask.

"Of course I'll come back," he says, kneeling down, resting his hand on my shoulder.

"But how will you find us? We don't have our phones."

Amos looks around. "How about we meet at that skate park in two hours?"

I look at the empty concrete pool overlooking the ocean, where shirtless skater dudes fly through the air. "Promise?" I ask.

He sticks out his pinky and links it with mine. "Promise."

41

AMOS

He's probably still sleeping. After all, it's what, midday? Or, better yet, he's probably passed out with the bottle of tequila between his legs. Those were fun times. When Louisa would come home from work and find him like that on the couch. I'd be in my room, pretending to be oblivious to the whole mess. Louisa would do her best to clean up the obvious evidence of the train wreck that was Clay's life, but New York City apartments are small, especially for us back in those days. There was no way to hide the sounds of their inevitable arguments when he'd finally sober up.

I guess if I knew the shit storm Louisa would throw at me when the buzz wore off, I'd keep drinking, too. I can't really blame him. Except that I do. Not so much for being a lousy alcoholic, or a mediocre painter, or even a fair-weather father. Not even for leaving. It was the way he did it. He seemed to just pick up and move to Los Angeles—a place that was so clearly the opposite of us—without ever looking back. Without any remorse.

I talk myself out of ringing the bell again. It's getting pathetic, and I'm not eleven years old anymore. I'm trying to figure out how I'm going to kill a couple of hours before we all meet back up, when I turn around, and there he is. Or a version of him, anyway. His hair is longer and grayer, and his skin is tanner, all of which somehow makes his eyes look greener. Or maybe it's just that for once they're not bloodshot. But hell, the day is still young.

What's more unrecognizable is the whole scene. He's returning from somewhere on a bicycle with a quaint wicker basket. Which means, inconceivably, he was up and out early in the day. Unless he's only now returning from last night? But he's in workout-type clothes, and the basket on the bike holds a bag of what appears to be groceries. Is it possible he really did get sober this time? As I try to make sense of it all, he must be doing the same, because it takes us the same number of seconds to greet each other questioningly.

"Hi, Dad," I manage at the same time that he says, "Amos? Wow! Hey!"

"I was in the neighborhood," I answer as ambiguously as possible. I watch him watching me, trying to determine if he knows that he's got a son on the run. But he seems to accept the unlikely circumstances more easily than one would expect. That's the thing about Clay. He exists in such a different dimension that, for better or worse, he never lets himself get too mired in the logistics of any particular situation. So instead of asking me what I'm doing here in California, at his door, or where my mother is, he simply says, "Would you like to come in?"

His house is posh yet bohemian—exactly what you'd expect from a trust-fund deadbeat with an artistic aesthetic. Smooth cement floors, a kitchen with new appliances I can't imagine he's ever used. There's not enough furniture in the place, but the pieces he does have are good—his father's original Eames chair, and the Le Corbusier lounge chair that he loved to pass out on in our old living room. Did he somehow manage to take that with him when he left? Or did Louisa send it to him when she exorcised every last bit of our old life? The place is littered with paint splatters, serapes, and surfboards. I study the space, trying to understand him, or maybe I'm just looking for traces of myself. I just need something to grab on to, to confirm that this man I haven't seen in years is connected to me in any real way at all.

Now that I'm inside, I can tell that Clay doesn't quite know what to do with me. In an effort to avoid his asking me too many questions, I throw Clay a bone and make some easy conversation.

"I like what you've done with the place," I offer innocuously.

"That's right—you haven't seen it since the remodel. Still moving things around here and there," he says, taking stock, and it's hard to tell with him if he's self-conscious or proud. He's hard to read, with his whiskey voice and that mischievous grin. No wonder Louisa fell for him. She can be such a fool.

"Yeah, it's only been, what, three years?" I say pointedly, because sometimes I just can't help myself.

FLYNN

"Are you sure you want to do this?" Neel asks me.

"Positive," I reply, without missing a beat.

Because I'm over being so me about everything. Of always being the one to sit on the bench with the chaperone while the other kids ride the roller coaster, or being the only one at summer camp too afraid to jump off the high dive. I don't know why I was such a cautious kid. I remember being eight years old on a trip to visit my dad in New York when he took me to see *Les Misérables* on Broadway for the first time. And as soon as the orchestra began to play the overture, my heart began to beat out of my chest. I ran out of the theater and into the lobby. Dad followed me, and I told him I was having a heart attack.

Turned out it was an anxiety attack. The first of many I'd have throughout my childhood. They sent me to some frigid shrink, who said I was probably just homesick. I doubted the diagnosis, because the anxiety continued even when I was back home with my mom. And then, when she was killed, it was like all my anxiety was confirmed. And I knew that the world really was as dangerous and callous and cruel as I'd always suspected it to be deep down in my bones.

It's the central truth that everyone tries to hide and lie about, especially to children. Like some grand conspiracy. I always knew different, but they tried to deny it, which made me feel crazy. But once Mom was gone, they couldn't deny it anymore, and I knew I had been right all along. Poppy's the same way—I can just tell. And now I'm torn because I want to shield her from it, too. But then I'd be just like them. And Amos always says the hottest fires in hell burn for hypocrites. We really have to figure out what to do about Poppy. I don't want her to be broken like me.

"Ow!" I shriek, overcome by the heat and throbbing in my nose from the needle prick.

The next thing I know, Neel's tongue is in my mouth, and my face is red and throbbing for an entirely different reason. I've never been kissed in public before. In fact, I usually find public displays of affection cringeworthy. But being kissed by Neel, in front of all these people, is thrilling and consuming in a way that makes me forget all about how gross it is when Bennett and Sabrina suck face for hours on the steps of the Met, and how annoying it is when Aisha and I practically have to pry them away from each other so we don't get a late slip every single morning.

"Feel better?" Neel asks when our lips finally part.

"Much," I reply, trying to will the rosiness out of my cheeks. I lightly touch the gold stud that now pierces the side of my nose. It feels tender and sore, but the tatted guy at the store assures me the pain will subside in a few hours. He's got about twenty piercings in his left ear alone, so I figure he knows what he's talking about.

"Can I get this?" Poppy comes over to me as I settle up at the cash register, holding a colorful hand-blown glass pipe.

"Do you know what that is?" Neel questions her, while privately cracking up.

"What is it?" Poppy answers innocently.

"Nothing, Poppy. Put it away. We're not going to waste our money on that," I say, grabbing her hand and dragging her out of the shop.

"You all right?" Neel asks as we emerge from the shop and into the glaring midday sun.

"Yeah," I lie. "I think the incense in there was starting to get to me." Because once we're back in the bright light of day, whatever brief thrill I felt from Neel's kiss feels fleeting, and I'm reminded once again of Amos's sudden absence.

I know he went to see Clay. What I don't know is why. Or why he didn't talk to me about it first—especially since he seemed so opposed to the idea when I mentioned it at the airport yesterday. I try to remind myself that not everything has to do with me, but part of me can't help but feel like Amos took off the way he did because of me. Or, more accurately, because of Neel and me. I know it seems childish, but I think it's possible that Amos felt left out, and taking off to see Clay like that was his way of leaving *me* out. Because even back when Amos and I used to tell each other absolutely everything, Clay was always a touchy subject.

It wasn't like Amos and I never talked about my mom or his dad. It was more like we had this unspoken understanding to tread lightly around the topic of our absent parents, each allowing the other to start those sensitive conversations. For me it was too raw, too recent—all that pain lingering too close to the surface. But for Amos it was different. I could never tell if that was because Amos was embarrassed by Clay, or at least the man Louisa continually painted him to be, or if in a strange way Amos revered his father. And as grateful as I was for our "understanding," I hated that he had something separate from me.

It's just that Amos can be so untouchable sometimes. It's like one minute he's right there, and just his very presence is everything you could ever need. Without making a big deal of it, he'll do these little things that show you he knows exactly who you are. Like when we see a movie, and there's a sad part we didn't expect, where maybe a parent dies or something, he'll always suggest we go for ice cream after, or give me dibs on the TV remote. It's just his way of letting me know that he knows when my throat tightens up and my heart feels like it's breaking all over again. And that makes me feel less alone. Every time Amos does something like that, he puts the pieces back together for me.

But then, the next minute, he'll do something cruel—like secretly apply to boarding school and leave without even a goodbye. Or disappear to see his estranged dad, and not even tell me where he's going.

"Holy shit!" Neel calls out. "Guess who just popped up in my news feed?" He flashes his phone, and there it is—a link from the *New York Post.* The Page Six headline reads: "On the Run," and there are pictures of Amos, Poppy, and me below.

43

AMOS

When Clay offered to make fresh juice with his newly procured produce from the farmers' market, I accepted in pure shock and morbid curiosity. In the entirety of my experience with my father, the only thing I'd seen him make was a stiff drink. Granted, the only thing I've ever seen my mom make for dinner is a reservation, but still, it was better than the nights when she had a work event and I was left alone with Dad, and dinner depended on if he remembered to eat at all.

So you can imagine my surprise when Clay unpacks a cloth sack full of fruits and vegetables I can't even identify, and proceeds to expertly prep them before feeding them into some steel contraption. Out comes a concoction of celery, wheatgrass (whatever that is), kale, cucumber, and various other veggies, which he splits between two cups. He hands one to me.

Clay raises his glass and says, "*Salud.*" He downs his completely, while I'm still eyeing mine dubiously. He waits for me to sample his specialty, so I man up and take a swig. It requires all my effort not to wince or gag as the grassy slime slides down my throat, but I smile graciously and nod in approval.

"That'll put some hair on your chest," Clay says, tossing his sly grin my way, and I still can't tell if he's suspicious of my arrival. Clay comes out from behind the white marble counter that divides the kitchen from the main living space, and settles onto the sofa.

"Why don't you have a seat?" he says, looking at me closely. This is it. He's going to lay into me for not returning any of his recent calls. Or worse. He knows I'm a fugitive. Shit. I sit down as instructed and brace myself for what's to come. But instead he picks up a guitar that's leaning beside the couch, and he nonchalantly starts to tune it. "So, Sonny, what're you doing out west?" he casually asks, without a note of concern. I have to make a critical decision—how honest am I willing to be?

"I had a layover," I answer, not totally lying. And again, strangely, that seems enough to satisfy him for at least the time being. I decide to change the subject and divert attention away from my unexpected LA appearance. I've learned that people, when given the opportunity to talk endlessly about themselves, usually take it. And Clay, it turns out, for all his idiosyncrasies and extravagances, is no exception.

All I have to do is ask him how life is treating him, and sit back as he launches into a soliloquy about how proud he is of the way his practice is evolving, and how dedicated he's been to nurturing it lately. I'm thinking, Good for him, he must be taking his twelve-step thing seriously. That would explain all the green juice. It turns out he's talking about his yoga practice. But hey, whatever works.

And just to indulge him a little bit, I act super enthralled, and keep asking questions, and sipping this disgusting drink, which I'm actually starting to enjoy. LA can be so insidious like that. At first, an eighty-degree December day seems appallingly unnatural, but watch out, because after a few hours of blue sky and wide empty beaches, you too will wish you were a yoga mat–toting, green juice–sipping dude strolling along Abbot Kinney in the City of Fallen Angels. That's the thing about LA—despite your initial impressions to the contrary, it's intoxicating. Like Clay's green juice. Or the man himself, for that matter.

When Clay invites me upstairs to check out the latest piece he's working on in his studio, I say yes a little too eagerly. Why am I worried about embarrassing myself in front of him? He leads me up the staircase to his open studio space. There are skylights above, and there's a glass wall that faces the beach, so it almost feels like we're floating above the sand. In the center of the room there's a giant slab of some kind of marble-like rock that's just beginning to be chiseled away. I follow him over to a drafting table at the side of the room, and he pulls a bunch of sketches out of a portfolio. And that's when I see it. Standing side by side, we have the exact same hands.

FLYNN

So we're missing. Officially. Not like we weren't missing before, but now it all feels much more real. This is bigger than us now—like an avalanche that keeps growing and can't be stopped. Jack and Louisa have gone public—we're national news. Guess the email we sent last night didn't ease their minds. That's okay. Let them worry. Let them care for once. Let them see that the kids are *not* all right. There's a tiny voice that's worrying if this will get me in trouble at school. And how will this look on college applications? But my heart is beating out of my chest, and despite the tiny voice, I just want to keep moving. Mostly because it seems impossible to stop.

I turn to Poppy. "The worst thing we could do is act suspiciously. Let's just be cool," I say, trying my best to heed my own advice.

"It's gonna be fine," Neel says, as he takes his baseball cap off his head and places it on Poppy's in an attempt to cover her up. "See? Incognito," he says. I sigh. It's not much, but it will have to do.

I wish I could call Amos right now. I need to tell him about the article in the *Post,* but of course I have no way of reaching him. I curse him for leaving us. We're not supposed to meet for another forty minutes, so Neel suggests we check out the farmers' market. We wait for the traffic to slow, and I take Poppy's hand as we all quickly dash across the street and toward the bustling crowds.

"Hey! You three! Stop right there," a voice calls out from behind us. We turn around, and a police officer walks over to us slowly, deliberately. I knew it. We're busted. She's tall and her stride is strong. And she's got her eyes fixed on Poppy and me. *Don't freak out, don't freak out, don't freak out.*

"What do you think you're doing?" she asks us.

"Um . . . ," Poppy mutters as she looks up at me, her eyes full of fear.

"You kids think you're above the law?" she asks pointedly as she takes a pen out of her shirt pocket.

"Officer—" I try to interject, my voice wavering.

"Jaywalking is a finable offense in this jurisdiction," she reprimands us. *Jaywalking? Seriously?* I think, relieved she doesn't recognize us.

"Apologies, Officer," Neel says, suddenly speaking in a British accent. "We're here on holiday. And we simply did not know."

"Please take pity," I pipe in, with just about the worst fake accent I've ever heard. I have to bite down on my tongue; otherwise I will burst out laughing.

The officer shakes her head. "You know, the point of the law is so that you don't get yourself killed."

"Yes. Of course. And we promise to follow it from now on," I say, my eyes desperately begging her to just let us off the hook.

She gives us each a once-over, then finally relents. "I'll let you off with a warning this time. But you kids need to be more careful. The drivers around here can be crazy."

"Thank you so much, Officer," I say, and quickly usher Poppy and Neel away from her and into the open market. I don't know how much longer my nerves can take this.

"Ohmygosh I thought she was going to arrest us," Poppy says.

"Nice accent," I say to Neel.

"What? I thought I sounded pretty legit! You, on the other hand . . ."

"How about we try to avoid any more run-ins with the law. That was seriously close." I try my hardest to shake off the *Post* story and the interaction with the police officer. *Just stay calm, Flynn,* I tell myself. *Everything's going to be fine.*

I walk past a stand where a woman is selling every berry imaginable, and I slip a strawberry into my mouth. Neel helps himself to the samples at the stalls wherever available—nut butters, artisanal honey, fresh-baked breads, and more. The air smells like kettle corn, and I finally start to breathe like a normal person again. As I browse the various booths, I find myself fidgeting with the new piercing on the side of my nose. I can't believe I actually did it. And by *it,* I mean something. *Anything.* I like touching it to remind myself that it's there. A real, tangible mark. Of what, I'm not quite sure—independence? Bravery? Rebelliousness?

It's funny, not like funny ha-ha, but I guess funny interesting, because I used to privately make fun of those girls who would come back to school after summer break and their hair would be dyed jet black or bright blue. Or the sweet girls who were in honors math with me at the lower school, and then all of a sudden were giving blow jobs in the bathroom at parties. You know, those girls who were so aggressively trying to shed one image for another. But I understand it now. Sometimes you have to destroy what was there in order to let something new emerge.

As I contemplate my own cause, I decide to do something else. I grab Neel and kiss him—trying to re-create the way he kissed me back at the piercing place. I can taste the hummus on his tongue. It feels even more exciting to kiss him out here in the open—in broad daylight. I decide to be even bolder, and open my eyes. His face is right there next to mine, his eyes gently shut. I wonder what he's thinking as he kisses me. What the people around us are thinking—if they're thinking about us at all. What must Poppy think? Poppy!

I pull away from Neel abruptly, accidentally biting his lip in the process. "Have you seen my sister?" I cry, frantically scanning the scene.

"She was with us a second ago," Neel offers, as if that's any consolation. My eyes search the crowds, but everything blurs, and the only thing I can feel is a giant pit in my stomach. Poppy is nowhere in sight.

POPPY

Holy moly, we're wanted. I've dreamed about being famous my whole life; I just never thought it would be for something like this. I really hope Rosie didn't see it. She'd be so worried—there aren't enough candles in Saint Patrick's Cathedral. This isn't good.

Even though Flynn was freaked out, she sure seemed to get distracted pretty easily by Neel. It's getting to be kind of gross. And I can't believe she wouldn't let me buy that little piece of colored glass I wanted. I added to our runaway fund, too, for the record. It's not like I don't have my own money. I get an allowance. Mom and Dad give me twenty dollars every week that I don't have an episode. I'm allowed to spend it on pretty much whatever I want. That's why it's called an *allowance.* After making me wait around that place for long enough, she sure rushed us out fast. It's fine by me. Aside from the pretty glass, I didn't really like that store. It kinda reminded me of the one next to the comic book shop on St. Mark's Place that Amos always takes me to. That place gives me the creeps, too.

Now Flynn's following Neel around this outdoor food fair–type thingy. I'm getting hungry, but no one has said anything about lunch. I'm trying to keep up with them, but my legs are shorter than theirs, and there are so many people, and carts, and dogs, and strollers.

I've almost caught up with Flynn when I spot the cutest little puppy I've ever seen. I bend down to pet the little guy, and just as I'm reaching out to rub behind his floppy little ear, he takes off! He just runs away! I start to chase him because I don't know who he belongs to, and he's headed out of the farmers' market and into the street. He's running away! Who knows what could happen? I've gotta go get him.

46

AMOS

So that happened. I saw my dad. Which doesn't necessarily need to be a thing. Except it was. Because this time felt different. Not because of the new-age LA bullshit. I mean, the dude invited me to a breathing workshop this afternoon. But because I was different. I don't need him to wipe my ass anymore, or make me macaroni and cheese, or take me to the park to teach me how to toss the ball back and forth. And since I wasn't constantly expecting those things from him, I wasn't disappointed. In the clarity of Clay's sobriety, I was actually able to see him. And who knows, maybe he could see me, too.

Just as I start to feel guilty for all of Clay's unreturned phone calls, I round the corner about a block from our agreed-upon meeting place, and there's Poppy, looking disoriented and oblivious. Instinctively, I race toward her. She spots me, and her face lights up.

"Amos!" she exclaims, running toward me.

"What are you doing? Where's Flynn?"

"She's right over . . ." Poppy looks around, as if realizing for the first time that she's alone. "I dunno," she says, suddenly perplexed.

"What do you mean, you don't know?" I say, alarmed.

"We were together . . . and then we weren't. And she and Neel—"

"They left you?" I scoff.

"Well, there was this cute puppy, and no one was looking after him . . . Oh! And we made the news!"

"Wait, what?"

"There you are!" I hear Flynn exclaim from across the street. She runs toward us, with that putz pulling up the rear.

Flynn grabs Poppy, kneels down, and imploringly asks, "Where were you?"

"No, Flynn, where were you?" I ask, pulling her up so we're standing face to face. It comes out pointed and like an accusation, which I'm happy about, because it's exactly how I mean it to sound.

"Shouldn't I be asking you the same thing?" Whenever Flynn attempts to sound indignant, it always comes off as immature instead. I study her for a second, shaking my head, and then I see it.

"What the hell is that?"

"What?"

"On your nose."

"None of your business," she snaps.

"Did you pay for it?" I press.

"Yeah."

"Well, then it's absolutely my business. How much did it cost?"

"Relax, Amos," she says. And then she hands me three measly twenty-dollar bills. That's it. Sixty dollars. That's all we have left.

"Are you *insane*? Flynn, you—"

"All right, guys," Neel interrupts. "Let's just put this all into perspective," he says, as if his perspective is anything I'd ever consider. All I want to do is bitch this kid out, and if it weren't for Poppy, I probably would.

47

FLYNN

What timing. I swear, Amos is so f-ing aggravating with his moral platitudes. Back in Neel's car, I tell him about the article, and he doesn't even freak out. He just looks at me straight on and says, "Guess they didn't take our email so well. Hate to say I told you so." Like I'm the dumbest person in the world. "Did you think Jack and Louisa would just wish us well, and say bon voyage? Come on, Flynn. Grow up."

Amos can be so self-righteous sometimes. I bet that's one of the reasons he left—he was so disgusted and disappointed with me and everyone else he knew in New York that he had to go find a whole new place filled with all new people he hadn't yet deemed fatally and irreversibly flawed. He has such fixed ideas of what's right and wrong, cool and uncool, interesting and banal. Doesn't he ever get tired of being so judgmental all the time? But the thing is, even after everything, I can tell you that when Amos is on your side, there's no better ally in the world.

Like at my piano recital two years ago. I was going to play Chopin's Scherzo No. 3, and Madame Locke (she insisted we call her Madame even though I know for a fact she was from Poughkeepsie, not Paris) had selected me to close the show. It sounds like more of an honor than it actually was, since most of her students are young kids. I guess as those things go, though, it was kind of a big deal. I tried not to make a whole to-do about it, but I was excited and nervous—mostly because Madame Locke had made the mistake of telling me that one of her little eight-year-olds had a father who sat on the admissions committee at Juilliard, and that he would be attending our recital in the Versailles Room at the St. Regis.

So I practiced and practiced, and even let Louisa take me to the fifth floor at Bergdorf's for a new party dress. "Something smart and sensible," she told her personal shopper. "But ladylike. And of course, age appropriate," she added. That evening I blow-dried my hair for once, and pinned it back in a half-up and half-down way I know my mother loved. I wore her locket, fastened tightly around my neck, for luck. But still I felt jittery butterflies in a way I always did when I was performing in front of other people.

The performances go in age order from youngest to oldest so the little ones can go home to bed during intermission. I felt sicker to my stomach with each ascending age group. By the time they got to the twelve-year-olds, I was sure I was going to puke. I scanned the crowd of proud parents and grandparents perusing the program and readying their cameras, looking for my own. But my dad and Louisa were nowhere in sight. *Mom would have been here,* I couldn't help but think, *front and center.* I tried not to let myself fall down this rabbit hole into the inevitable well of tears that lay below. I told myself to think of something else—anything else—fast. Like the first few bars of my piece. And then all of a sudden I realized . . . it was gone. All of it. I couldn't even remember what piece I had prepared for the evening.

I broke out into a cold sweat. Feeling like I was about to faint, I decided to bolt. At the very least, I could show Juilliard the professional courtesy of not passing out in front of everyone. Everything was blurry, but somehow I made my way from my seat in the second row out the back doors. As I emerged into the much cooler air of the lobby, I felt a hand grab me. I turned around. It was Amos.

"You came!" I breathed.

"Wouldn't miss it," he reassured me. "Besides, *Real Housewives* is a repeat tonight."

I smiled.

"What are you doing out here?" he questioned. "You're not a flight risk, are you?"

"They're not coming, are they?" I had to know.

"Louisa got called in. Something about an artist having a meltdown."

"Story of life," I replied, sounding so bitter it surprised me. "And my dad?"

"We came together. But he's still outside, finishing a call."

I struggled to take steady, laborious breaths.

“You’re going to kill it,” Amos said as he stared knowingly into my eyes. And then he did the funniest thing. He started humming my piece and prancing around the lobby. He knew it by heart. And with that, it all came rushing back to me. I threw my arms around him and felt the color come back into my cheeks.

I went back to the doors of the ballroom and peered in. Ava Adahm was finishing her sonata. I was next. I kissed Amos on the cheek and marched down the aisle toward the risers. And as I did, I heard Amos call out behind me, “You got this, kid.” Amos is not just a good friend to have. He’s the best friend. And sometimes I wish we could go back to a time when it was simple enough for me to just call him my brother.

48

POPPY

"What about this one?" I say to Flynn as I hand her a bedazzled yellow-and-gold dress to try on.

"That's a sari. Very cool, but probably not the right look for the night," she tells me.

We've torn apart Neel's stepmom's closet for the past hour—like we're looking for a hidden treasure. Neel's stepmom must be really small for a grown-up, because some of her dresses are even too short for Flynn! Flynn said she wanted to wear something festive to Neel's friend's party tonight, and even though I think she looks so perfect in everything, she claims she still hasn't found "the one." The only reason I even get to go to the party is because Bebe is off, and no one wanted to be stuck staying home with me. And anyway, at this point we're so far past breaking Mom and Dad's rules, what's one more?

Flynn slips on a navy-blue strapless dress and looks at

herself in the mirror. She messes with her hair, stands on her tippy-toes, and checks herself out from just about every angle. She sighs, annoyed. I've never seen her like this. Not over a dress, at least.

"What do you think?" she asks me.

"The maybe pile?" I say, even though I know she'd rather it go in the no pile. I continue to dig through the costume jewelry that's spilling out of the drawers. I've got about a hundred bangles clanking on my wrists, and so many strands of pearls that the weight is starting to strain my neck. I put on a pair of bug-eye sunglasses and stand next to Flynn in the mirror. I rest my hand on my hip the way all the famous people do when they're on the red carpet, but I know I'm not fooling anyone. I'll never be the girl with the super-sparkly dress.

Usually I sit in my mom's dressing room while she's getting ready for an auction. While she debates which black blouse to wear with which black slacks, she tells me about the art she'll be selling that night. There's nothing my mom loves more than beautiful things. Sometimes I think she's disappointed that I'm not beautiful the way she is. She always tells me that I'm smart. And unique. But she never says beautiful.

Flynn holds up a tiny red party dress, and says, "Can you imagine Louisa in this?"

"I think my mom would die," I say, and suddenly it's like there's no air in the room. I can be such an idiot! No wonder I wasn't invited to Tatiana's sleepover party. "Not die," I say, freaking out. "I just meant . . ."

Flynn just smiles and says, "It's okay, Poppy." But how could it possibly be okay? I used the words *mom* and *die* in the same sentence. I feel the tears welling in my eyes, and I know I shouldn't be the one crying because I'm the one with the mom who's still alive, but I can't stop them from coming out. I am trying to be better about controlling my emotions, but it's not easy. Flynn comes over and puts her arm around me.

"I didn't mean it. I really didn't."

"Let's not cry over an ugly red dress," she says, gently stroking my hair. I wish I could have met Flynn's mom. I know from the framed picture of her Flynn keeps on her desk that they look alike. Flynn's mom doesn't look anything like my mom. She's more . . . natural. The picture is really pretty—it was taken at Flynn's birthday party when she was a little girl. She's about to blow out the candles, and her mom is right next to her—smiling as Flynn closes her eyes, about to make her wish. Sometimes Flynn talks about her mom. Like, I know that she used to play the piano, too, and that she grew vegetables in their backyard, and that she liked to ride horses. I want to know more about her mom, but I don't know if it's okay to ask. I've never known anyone with a dead mom.

We keep searching the closet, and just as I think we're never going to find something, I see it. "Flynn, this is it! This is the one."

FLYNN

As we walk barefoot down the beach to the party just a few houses over, I try my hardest not to pull at my dress, but it's so short and so tight that it keeps riding up my legs. I've never worn anything like this—something so unabashedly sexy, something that requires so much . . . confidence. All the other dresses I tried on felt like costumes with their fringe and fake jewels. But this one is simple. Just black. Just short. Just tight.

"I can hear the music!" Poppy says as she skips up to me. She looked so fragile after that silly dead-mom comment, so I'm happy to see she's moved on from it. She can be so sensitive sometimes. It's what I love about her, but it's also what worries me most. How is she possibly going to cope with growing up, with junior high school, and now with Dad and Louisa's divorce?

Of course, I would never tell her about the pang in my chest that I feel whenever people make stupid comments about their moms. It's worse at school—lately it feels like every day I have to hear everyone complaining about how much they hate their mothers, how they're ruining their lives, how they just don't understand. I know, I know. We're teenage girls. Defying your mother is some rite of passage on the path to becoming a woman. I wonder if I would fight with Mom now, if she were still here. Back then she was my best friend. She was my favorite person in the whole world. But back then was a while ago.

"It's the next house," Neel says, gently resting his hand on my lower back.

"And you're sure it's okay for us to come?" I ask.

"For sure. It's going to be chill. You'll see—Sawyer super gets it," Neel reassures me.

"Super . . . ," Amos says ironically, a few steps behind. Neel pretends like he doesn't even hear him, and I decide to do the same. I take a deep breath as I dust the sand off my feet and slip on my Converse. Because tonight isn't about Amos, or dead moms, or living in the past. Tonight is the night I lose my virginity to Neel Khan.

AMOS

This party is a shit show, and I can't say I'm surprised. I immediately take Poppy's hand and hold on to it tightly. I know she wants to prove to us that she can hang with the older kids, but I also know that she gets scared in big crowds. As we make our way through the house, I realize I've already lost Flynn and Neel, which I can't say I'm surprised about, either. I'm sure they assumed that I would be babysitting Poppy tonight. Which is cool with me, considering she's probably the most interesting person here.

I scan the crowd—and I'm mildly amused and offended by the scene, which, to be fair, is how I am at most social gatherings these days. Sawyer's house is all right. Unlike Neel's place, it looks like people actually live here. There are stains on the carpet, the furniture is dated, and there are ugly Christmas decorations everywhere. There's a golden retriever with a Santa hat roaming around that seems to be the designated mascot for the evening.

"Amos?" Poppy says, pulling me down to her ear level.

"Yeah?"

"I kind of gotta go . . . you know?" Obviously. I don't even try to look for Flynn for this task. I lead Poppy down the hallway and ask a girl in passing where the nearest bathroom is. She points to the last door on the left. I turn the handle, but it's locked. We wait. And when the door opens, a guy in one of those dumb slouchy beanies and a girl in a dress that looks just as desperate as the one Flynn is wearing emerge, inconspicuously wiping their noses.

I look at Poppy, who is thankfully oblivious. What were we thinking, bringing her here? I poke my head into the bathroom to make sure they didn't leave behind any party favors, and then assure Poppy that I'll be waiting for her right outside. She nods and goes in. Once I hear the door lock, I shove my hands in my pockets and lean my head against the wall. Maybe I should just take Poppy back to Neel's now.

"You in line?" I turn to see a girl with long red hair and thick-framed glasses that make her hazel eyes look like they take up half her face.

"Just waiting for someone," I reply. This girl looks like she's too smart to be at a party this dumb. I watch her as she pulls a joint out of her jean jacket and lights up. She raises her eyebrows, offering it to me. I look at the bathroom door, still closed, and quickly take a hit.

"Thanks," I say, exhaling. After a minute, Poppy reemerges, and the girl with the red hair and the glasses looks all sorts of confused. I just shrug as Poppy takes my hand, and we continue on through the party. The house somehow got even more packed in the past ten minutes, and as we push our way through into the kitchen, it strikes me that it really doesn't matter if you're in an apartment in Manhattan, a dorm room in Massachusetts, or a beach house in Malibu: all high school parties are exactly the same. I can't help but laugh at the irony. This whole time I've been fooling myself, thinking I could escape high school by changing the scenery. High school is high school. No matter where you are.

"Punch?" some dude offers.

"Yes, please," Poppy says, reaching for the red Solo cup. I quickly intercept, grabbing it out of her hands.

"No punch, Poppy." I spot an unopened bottle of Martinelli's apple cider on the counter, and grab it. "C'mon. Let's go outside." We go onto the deck where the smokers and stoners are situated. I find a corner for us, pop open the bottle, and offer her the first swig.

"I'm going to pretend that it's champagne," she says. She takes another sip—a big one—and then lets out an involuntary burp—also a big one. She grins from ear to ear, and I do, too. I wonder how she's been doing at school this year. I know it's not easy for a kid like her. When she was really little, Louisa must have dragged her around to every specialist on the entire island of Manhattan, but it turns out there's no exact diagnosis for a girl who's crippled by anxiety, fear, and obsessive-compulsive disorder, and certainly no miracle cure. I know my mom fixates on all the ways Poppy doesn't fit her vision of the perfect family. But what Louisa never sees is that it wasn't until Poppy was born that we even became a family. She's our glue. I watch as she takes in the scene.

Finally, she turns to me and says, "It's no Disneyland, but it'll do."

"You know, you're something else, Poppy."

"Is that a good thing?"

"It's the best thing."

"I really missed you, Amos," she says, and it almost sounds like she could cry.

"I really missed you, too," I tell her.

"No one else gets me the way you and Flynn do. The kids at school think I'm weird." She looks up at me, and my heart breaks for her.

"They think I'm weird at my school, too," I reply.

"Yeah, right."

"It's true. But you have to remember that weird is good. Weird means you have personality. Weird means you're not like everyone else."

"But why can't you be weird back in the city? Then at least we could be weird together," she asks.

"I can't come back, Poppy. I just . . . can't. I'm really sorry I left. But you know it has nothing to do with you, right?"

"Was it because of Mom and Dad?"

"It's kind of hard to explain."

"Why is everyone always telling me that?" She deflates.

Poppy is looking at me like I have the power to fix everything. And I wish I could for her. But I can't. So instead I put my arm around her and lift up the bottle.

"To us," I say.

Just then, the girl from the bathroom line walks by. She takes one look at Poppy and smiles. How could you not?

"I like your necklace," she says to her.

"Thanks," Poppy replies, twirling Neel's stepmother's fake pearls. "I like your glasses," Poppy tells her.

"Thanks. I'm Lucy."

"I'm Poppy, and this is my brother, Amos."

"Nice to meet you . . . officially," I say, extending my hand to her.

51

POPPY

Amos is making small talk with Lucy. She tells him she's a freshman at Brown University, and still figuring out what her major will be. They're going on and on about an "open curriculum," whatever that is, and the crazy thing is, they don't seem bored at all. I have to go to the bathroom again, but I can tell Amos doesn't want to leave Lucy. So I offer to go by myself. He asks me if I'm sure, and I say, "Sure, I'm sure." I walk back inside and tell myself that all I have to do is go right down the same hallway as before. Last door on the left. Lucky for me, there's no line this time.

Afterward, as I walk back through the house, I stop when I see Flynn, sitting close to Neel on the couch. She looks strange, and it's not the dress or her short hair. She seems like she's busy, so I don't go over and say hi. I look outside and see Amos and Lucy still talking—where am I supposed to go? I walk into the kitchen, take an empty plastic red cup, and help myself to some of the punch. It tastes sweet and kind of weird. I wait for a second to see if I feel any different. But I feel exactly the same. So I decide to take a few more sips. And then a few more. Slowly, things around me get kind of fuzzy. I start to sway back and forth, like I'm on a boat.

"Yo! Runaway!" I hear someone shout. I turn around and see Shappy. "What do you got there?" he asks, eyeing my drink.

"My brother said it's okay," I fib.

"Somehow I doubt that," Shappy says, taking the cup out of my hand. "Come with me." And because the room is really starting to spin, I let Shappy lead me away.

52

FLYNN

Neel and I are crammed on a couch, but I don't mind the proximity. He's chatting with his friends, and I'm just sort of sitting here, trying not to think about what's going to happen later. But of course it's all I can think about. Someone else tries to squish onto the sofa, so I scoot even closer to him.

"Maybe I should sit on your lap," I suggest. I ease myself onto Neel's lap and put my arm around him like it's something I do all the time. He smiles at me, and I realize that after tonight, everything will be different. Neel Khan will always be my first. He's a good candidate—he's cute and sweet. The buildup has been there for a while, and because of the geography, I won't have to worry too much about the aftermath. It's low stakes. And most of all, it will be over with, which, according to the girls at school, is the most important part.

A guy in a Santa hat approaches and says, "*Feliz Navidad,* motherfuckers." He opens his palm, revealing a handful of pills.

"What is it?" I ask.

"Who knows? That's the point," Santa says.

Neel grabs a pill, and so I grab one, too. I swallow it quickly—if I give myself any time to deliberate, I know I'll back out. And I've already come this far.

"Barlow, you continue to surprise me," he says.

And I stand up and grab Neel's hand, pulling him off the couch. We start dancing closely, and I don't care who's watching. Maybe it's that I'll never see anyone here again; maybe it's the dress; maybe it's the unmarked mystery pill. But right now I'm willing to take the leap.

53

AMOS

Lucy's pretty cool, for an LA girl. We've been talking about random shit for a while now—like how she recently got into transcendental meditation, and how her roommate at Brown is some born-again who eats Kraft Mac & Cheese every morning for breakfast. Usually the more time I spend talking to a girl, the less I like her, but Lucy's smart and she knows it. Maybe it's the weed kicking in, but I'm starting to think that I should make a move.

"You should come to Providence sometime—check out campus," Lucy says with a slight smile as she interlocks her fingers with mine. I agree too quickly, sounding like the high school kid I am. And why not? I don't need to play games with this girl. One thing's for certain, I am sick and tired of playing games.

Out of the corner of my eye, I see Poppy teeter outside, with Shappy trying to hold her up.

"Dude, think you better take her home," Shappy says.

"Amos . . . I don't feel so good," Poppy mumbles as I rush over to her. Her eyes are unfocused, and she looks out of it. Is she drunk?

"I found her by the punch bowl," Shappy informs me.

"Thanks, man," I say, and turn to Poppy. "You need water." But it's too late. She throws up—everywhere. "It's okay . . . you're okay," I tell her as I hold her hair and stroke her back. "That's good. Get it all out."

"Are you mad at me?" she asks as she lifts her head up, her voice sounding so small.

"Of course not. Come on, let's get you home." I lift her up and carry her inside. I nod to Shappy, grateful. Lucy follows, which I'm fine with. Girls usually know what to do in these kinds of situations, and it's not like Flynn is anywhere to be found.

I push through the crowds with Poppy in my arms, and try to ignore the inane "party foul" comments as we pass. We make our way through the house and nearly bump into Flynn—or, rather, she nearly stumbles into us. Neel's got his hands all over her, and they look high as hell. As we stand in the foyer, all the chaos of the party quiets, and Flynn and I just stare at each other. Finally her eyes fall on Poppy, who looks pale and weak, and like she may throw up again.

"Poppy, are you okay?" Flynn cries out.

"I think I had too much punch," Poppy says to Flynn.

"You gave her punch? What the fuck, Amos?" Flynn yells at me.

"Are you kidding me right now?" I say to her, seething.

"Yo, man, she didn't do anything," Neel says in Flynn's defense, getting a little too close to me.

"Exactly! She didn't *do* anything. Where have you been, Flynn? You've been so busy following this clown around that it didn't occur to you to check in on our little sister?"

"It looks like you got a bit distracted yourself," Neel says, gesturing to Lucy.

I swear, I can't handle this guy anymore. "Why don't you stay out of this, pal."

"I'm just trying to help you guys out here," Prince Freaking Charming says.

"Yeah, you've been real helpful," I reply, taking an aggressive step toward him.

"Whoa, dude. You've been a dick since you got here," Neel says. "And you've been treating Flynn like shit, too."

I swear, if I didn't have my little sister in my arms I would punch this kid in the face right here. But instead we just stand there. Staring each other down. I'm apoplectic, and Flynn can feel it. "I'm taking Poppy back to the house," I announce coldly.

"I'm coming with you," Flynn insists.

"Don't bother."

"Amos, I want to—" She tries to follow, but I turn around.

"I mean it, Flynn. I got this. We don't want you there." I glance at Poppy, tears welling in her eyes. Lucy's disappeared, and that's probably for the best. This night has turned into a disaster of epic proportions, and I have a feeling it's not even close to over.

"Come on," Neel says, taking Flynn by the hand. "You don't need this."

Flynn just stands there frozen, while I take Poppy and head toward the door without looking back.

FLYNN

"Did that just happen?" I ask, taking a seat on the steps behind me.

"Yeah, your stepbrother's kind of the worst," Neel answers, even though it was really more of a rhetorical question.

I put my head in my lap and curl my knees into my chest, turning myself into a ball and hoping that makes everything disappear, even though it doesn't. Neel puts his hand on my back and gently rubs it in a sweet effort to console me.

"It's going to be okay. Don't worry," he says. I want to believe him, but in this moment I realize how little Neel really knows about me. I know he's just genuinely trying to be nice. He's been nothing but great since we got to LA and shat all over his winter-break plans, so when he asks if there's anything he can do, I tell him that I'd really just love another drink.

I know I'm messed up from whatever that pill was, but it's beyond that—it's like nothing feels real. I look down at my hands, my legs, my feet, but everything seems distorted, fuzzy. I want to run back to the house to see Poppy, but Amos's words won't stop echoing in my head. *We don't want you there.* And I know he means it. Maybe they're better off without me. Somehow I've turned into an emotional hurricane—destroying everything around me. I glance around the party full of strangers, and everyone blurs into one confused mess. I need to hold on to something—anything.

Neel comes back with a beer. It tastes cold and bitter, and it actually makes me feel a little better. "Your sister's going to be all right. There's nothing you can do now anyway," he says. And I guess he's right. He leans into me, and we kiss. It feels good to be touched. To feel wanted.

And so I look at Neel and say, "Do you wanna go somewhere quiet?"

AMOS

I'm sitting on the cold floor of Neel's sister's bathroom, cradling Poppy in my arms. Fortunately, she's gotten all the alcohol out of her system, but I can tell she's still fighting sleep. How did we get here? I'm sure we must look a little ridiculous—after all, Poppy is approaching the point where she'll be too big for me to hold. She'll be ten on her next birthday, and then she'll be a preteen. It's hard for me not to always imagine her as a baby. But not just any baby. The baby who brought us together and made us a family.

Before Poppy arrived, Flynn and I still felt kind of like distant cousins. People who were allegedly tied, but the relation seemed forced, or just too abstract to feel any true connection. Then Poppy was born. And suddenly we were siblings. When Flynn visited from California, we would take turns doting on our new baby sister as if she were our own personal doll. We would make believe we were her parents, a game that continued for years.

Holding her in my arms now, I can't help but feel like I let her down. Her breath is heavy, and her body is limp. She's finally found her way to sleep. I tuck her safely into bed and head downstairs. There's something I have to do. I go into the kitchen, pick up the phone, and dial one of the only numbers I know by heart.

56

FLYNN

This isn't real. Except that it is. It's happening, but it's not happening. Or, rather, it's happening to someone else. Because even though I was the one who wanted to go upstairs, and it was my dress that Neel Khan took off, and my bra he unhooked, and, as much as I can see, those are most definitely my Converse lying next to the bed, it's like it's all happening to someone else. I know that it's me lying here with a boy I've had a crush on since last summer, but somehow it's like I'm hovering off in the corner someplace, watching it all.

"You good?" Neel asks me as he brushes my hair back and looks down at me sweetly. I respond with a kiss, because all I can think really is, *So this is sex?* And I can't help but feel massively misled. Because it's not at all what it looks like in the movies. And I don't feel at all like how I thought I would feel, but maybe that's the pill talking. Because now that I think about it, I really don't feel much of anything. Except for maybe a little discomfort, and mild impatience for it to all be over. I wonder briefly if Neel's doing it all wrong, or, more likely, maybe I'm all wrong, because this certainly doesn't feel . . . right. There are no sparks flying, no fireworks, no all-encompassing passion. The whole thing is clumsier and more mechanical than I think it's supposed to be.

Don't get me wrong—I'm not here against my will. This is what I wanted. Or what I thought I wanted, anyway. Especially after the blowout with Amos downstairs. But now that I'm here and it's actually happening, I don't really want it at all. Still, when Neel smiles at me like this is the best thing ever, for some reason I smile back. I'm starting to seriously question what all the fuss was about, and why I was in such a rush. Do I get a take-back? But even though I know pretty much nothing about sex, I know enough to know that I don't.

The door bursts open, and two tipsy teenagers I don't know topple in. They tear at each other's clothes for a good ten seconds before they realize the room is already in use. Neel valiantly attempts to cover my bare body. "Dude! Get out!" he shouts, scaring them away. He turns back to me. "Sorry about that," he says as he catches his breath. "Do you want to stop?" I partly wonder if Neel and I can just call it quits and be done. But instead I shake my head, because the last thing I want to be is a tease. "You know, I've thought about you a lot," he says as he kisses my neck and gently runs his fingers through my hair, and I know he is trying so hard to do everything right.

Thankfully, it's all over pretty quickly, and then we just kind of lie there. I suddenly feel so naked, and all I want is to put my dress back on and run home. But the thing is, my dress is all the way on the other side of the room, and I don't even know where home is anymore. I feel my eyes welling with tears, and I try my hardest to swallow them. I cannot be the girl who cries after she loses her virginity.

"What are you thinking?" Neel asks, breaking the silence.

"Nothing," I lie. I'm thinking I want my clothes. I'm thinking I need to be alone. I'm thinking I've made a mistake. "I'm just going to use the bathroom—freshen up."

"I'll wait for you," Neel says, slipping back into his jeans.

"You don't have to—really. I'll be down in a few."

"All right," he says, somewhat reluctantly. He kisses me on the cheek and then looks at me, trying to get a read, but it's no use. "You sure you're okay?" he asks. I nod, encouraging him to leave already.

Once I'm alone, I look for my dress in the dark and find it balled up on the floor. I zip it back up and sit on the edge of the bed. *You are not going to cry,* I tell myself as tears silently stream down my face. *You are not crying.*

57

AMOS

The sun is coming up, and she's still not home. I'm sitting here at Neel's kitchen table, and I've been up all night. I feel like such a fool for letting her get away with this for this long. I mean, if she wanted to live out some Bonnie and Clyde fantasy with that bozo, that's one thing, but I shouldn't have let Poppy and me get dragged along for the ride. And now this little charade of hers has gone on long enough. I don't know what she was trying to accomplish, but running away from a family vacation, going off grid, and staying out all night with a delinquent surfer dumbass is taking it too far. If it was a cry for attention Flynn was after, I've heard it loud and clear. Congratulations, Flynn, we're all watching now.

And then there she is. Flynn stands at the glass door in last night's dress, barefoot with her shoes in her hand. I know how crappy she must feel from her walk of shame. Call me cruel, and maybe I am, but I want to let her sit in it. The girl standing at the door is not my Flynn. And maybe that's the problem. She was never my Flynn. Never could be my Flynn. We don't belong to each other. None of us. Clay could up and leave for California, just like I up and left for school. Jack and Louisa can split this family apart. The divorce is sure to be a real shit show—once all is said and done, there'll be nothing left of the family we thought we were anyway.

Flynn tries the glass door again, but it won't budge. I know because I locked it myself. I also know I should get up and open it for her, but I'm not sure I want to. So she stands there—looking at me. And I stare right back at her. And we both know that there is so much more than this glass wall between us now.

58

FLYNN

He's such an ass. Amos is enjoying this way too much. Suddenly I'm wishing I had stayed at Sawyer's. When I finally went downstairs last night, I found Neel in the living room, stoned and watching *Elf* with the stragglers still at the party. I joined them on the sofa, but I couldn't get into the movie. My mind was somewhere else. I finally stopped fighting sleep and let myself drift off. Eventually, Neel must have crashed, too, because when I woke up later, the sun was starting to come up, and he was there sleeping next to me. I contemplated waking him, but decided to slip out instead. He certainly didn't need to witness this. And it's already worse than I even expected.

I mean, is Amos just going to leave me standing out here all day? *Nice, Amos, real nice.* As if I don't already feel shitty enough. Isn't it just like him to rub my nose in it? He holds me in his unrelenting gaze. Always so moralistic. I wonder what the altitude is like up there on his high horse. But because I can't let him get away with feeling so smug and self-satisfied, I adopt an air of self-confidence, even though I'm feeling anything but. I steel myself to be stranded, standing out here for the long haul, but just as I do, Amos gets up.

"Well, well," he says, all indignant as he slides the glass door open without officially making eye contact with me. "Look what the cat dragged in."

"What's your problem, Amos?" I fire back, trying not to let my voice crack.

"I don't have a problem."

"Right."

"You know what? I take it back. I do have a problem," he says. And then, outrageously: "You. You're my problem, Flynn."

"Excuse me?"

"You've always been my problem."

I've been wanting to talk, I mean really talk, to Amos for so long—why does it have to be happening now? When I'm standing here, already at such a distinct disadvantage. In this stupid dress, with my body aching, my head throbbing, and a hunger in my stomach that I feel too ill to satisfy. Still, I'm not about to let the opportunity slide. So I ask him, "What's that supposed to mean?"

"From the second you showed up in New York like a sad, lost little mouse in the big city—"

"No one asked you to take me under your wing."

"No one thanked me, either."

"Is that what this is about? You don't feel like you've been properly exalted? I wasn't aware that I was such a charity case. So is that it? That's why you left? I was too big of a burden?"

"You know why I left."

"No, I don't, actually. Because we've never talked about it."

"Don't play innocent, Flynn. It's a little late for that."

"Fine. You want to talk? Let's talk."

"Whatever," Amos says dismissively, looking down.

"Don't whatever me. Suddenly you have nothing to say? Let's hear it, Amos. I can take it—"

"Forget it. It doesn't matter. None of it matters. They're on their way."

"What do you mean? Who?" I ask.

"Aliens. Who do you think? Jack and Louisa."

My heart drops, and all the air escapes my chest. *"What?"*

"I called them. They're coming to get us."

"Yeah, right." He can't be serious.

"They land at LAX later today."

Holy shit. He is serious. Everything deflates. My cheeks sting as if this slap in the face were as real as it feels. So not only are Amos and I not on the same team, but he's gone and unilaterally changed the rules, and apparently now we're playing for keeps.

"Why would you do a stupid thing like that?"

"Because, Flynn, it's all over."

"Now it is," I say, feeling like the whole world is crashing down around me. "But it didn't have to be."

"I'm tired of pretending this divorce isn't happening. I'm tired of denying reality."

"That's ironic," I reply. "I can't believe you would do this to us."

"I'm sorry you'll have to cut your lovefest short. But I'm sure you and Neel will—"

"No, Amos. I can't believe you would do that to *us*. You, me, and Poppy."

"We'll be okay. You'll move back to the Bay Area. You fit in better there anyway. I'll be done with school soon enough. And . . ." His voice trails off.

"And what about Poppy?"

I have Amos there. He tenses his brow—his face is stricken with guilt. For the first time this morning, his humanity is showing, and I can tell he did what he did out of spite. He didn't properly think it through, and now he's run the clock. It's over.

"Poppy will be okay," he says. But I know he doesn't believe it at all.

"Amos, you and I both know what happens to her when they get divorced."

"But, Flynn, it was inevitable. You and I, we couldn't have protected her from it together any better than we could have apart."

"She's going to be crushed."

Amos nods, and then we're silent for a long time. What have we done?

"Who's going to tell her?" I ask finally.

"I called them. I'll do it," he says, resigned.

"We can do it together. When do Jack and Louisa get in?"

"We have until seven tonight to face the reckoning," Amos says with a sigh.

This really does feel like the end of the road. But even after everything, I'm still not ready to let go. I look outside; the sun is shining. "You know, it's so early. We still have all day."

Amos thinks about it for a moment. "One last hurrah?"

"The three of us."

POPPY

I'm having a dream. I'm on the merry-go-round in Central Park. Except it's not the merry-go-round in Central Park. It's the Ferris wheel at the Santa Monica Pier. Except Flynn and Neel wouldn't take me on the Ferris wheel. And I'm not at the pier. I'm in a strange room. And it's not me that's spinning. It's the room. And it's not a dream. I feel sick, like I may throw up again, but I don't remember where I am, or where the bathroom is. I try to open my eyes, but my lids feel too heavy.

"Popsicle . . . you awake?" I can't remember the last time Amos called me that, but it still makes me smile. When I manage to open my eyes, I see Amos and Flynn hovering over me. Flynn's eyes are a little red and puffy, and I want to hug her and tell her that whatever it is, it's going to be okay, but my mouth is too dry to speak.

"Wanna go to Disneyland?" Flynn asks.

"For real?" I must still be dreaming. But they nod. It's really

happening! I jump up from the bed and squeeze them both so tightly.

"I guess that's a yes?" Amos says.

It doesn't take us long to get dressed since we only have our plane clothes. My head still hurts, but I'm too excited to care. I'm in the kitchen eating my second piece of toast, which Amos promises will help me feel better, when I ask Flynn how much longer Neel is going to be. I wanna leave already.

"That guy is not coming with us," Amos insists.

"Fine by me," Flynn answers as she zips up her backpack. "Today's about us. If we leave soon, we can be gone before he wanders back. You got all your stuff packed up, Pops?"

I double-check that I've got my camera in my bag. "Got it!" I say. "But how are we going to get there?" I wonder. And I seem to have stumped them. I can feel the day falling apart before it's even begun.

"Wait a second," Flynn says. She looks around the kitchen, and her eyes fall on a key rack hanging on the wall. "Who has a pen?" she asks. Amos opens a bunch of drawers until he pulls out a blue Sharpie and a pad of Post-its. He tosses them across the center island to Flynn, and she jots down a note. "Well, I think this qualifies as the biggest IOU ever."

"You can't be serious?" Amos says.

"What? We'll obviously bring the car back, and repay him for everything." She grins mischievously as she pulls Neel's credit card out of his wallet, which is resting on the counter. "Including this."

"You're insane." Amos shakes his head.

"Come on!" We follow Flynn through the laundry room.

She opens a door to a garage with so many sports cars, it looks like we've stepped into a James Bond movie.

Flynn clicks the button on the key, and the lights of a fancy black car flicker. "Bingo," she says.

"A Maserati?" Amos shrugs. "Don't mind if we do." As he turns on the engine, Flynn and I hop into the car. The garage door slowly inches its way up, and we zoom out onto Pacific Coast Highway.

60

FLYNN

I don't know if I want to scream or cry or laugh at this point. I'm so tired that I'm past the point of actually feeling tired. My eyes burn, my throat aches, and every bone in my body feels wrecked. It's almost hard to believe last night happened. But of course it did. All of it. And I feel . . . Well, I don't know how I feel. It's weird.

I flip down the passenger-side visor and look at myself in the tiny mirror. I brush my wind-blown hair out of my face and stare back at myself. Do I look different? More like a woman? Like a non-virgin? I guess a part of me is relieved that the whole mess is over. All the buildup, the wondering, the shying away from lunchtime conversations. All because I did this one thing. I flip the visor back up.

What will I tell the girls at school? I can already hear the whispers: "Flynn Barlow ran away, and lost her virginity at a party in LA." And it's not like there's anything so wrong with what happened, but now, the morning after, it doesn't feel like there was anything so right, either. Somehow, I got so caught up in the idea of having sex that I forgot about the most important part—my heart. Maybe that's why it feels so empty right now. Why didn't I wait for someone I love, and who loves me, too? And I like Neel. But now that he's seen me—and I mean really seen me—it doesn't feel like he knows me at all. Maybe I won't tell the girls at school anything, considering I'm probably moving away anyway. I break out into a cold sweat and put my head in my hands.

"Are you gonna throw up, too, Flynn?" Poppy pipes in from the backseat.

"Do you need me to pull over?" Amos asks. I shake my head. He turns his attention back to the road. Miraculously, he doesn't seem as utterly exhausted as I am.

"I'm okay, Poppy. I promise," I assure her. I can't be the thing that gets in the way of today. Because after today, this will all be over. I know we can't run forever. But that doesn't mean there isn't a part of me that wishes we could.

Amos redirects the air-conditioning vent to face me, and the blast of cool air makes me feel like I can breathe again.

"Thanks," I say to him.

"You'll feel better soon."

I nod, wanting to believe him. I hated seeing him so angry earlier. I hated being so angry. It wasn't any way for us to really talk. Not when we've waited this long. And the crazy thing is, even though I've been having pretend conversations with Amos in my head for the past six months, I still don't know what I would want to say to him.

Sure, I drafted about a hundred emails to him while he was at Andover. But there was never the right way to say, *Hey, Amos! About that time we kissed . . . weird, right?!* Or, *Amos, what if we just forget about what happened?* I'd think about hitting send, but then I'd remember that leaving the state of New York seemed like a better option to him than spending one more night living across the hall from me. I know I've never understood boys, but I thought I understood Amos. When he left, it was like a whole new kind of loss in my life. Why couldn't I just say, *Dear Amos, I love you. And I have no idea what that means*?

61

AMOS

I have to admit, this Maserati is pretty damn sweet. After spending the past two days stuck in the backseat of Neel's Land Rover, it feels nice to be behind the wheel. To be in control. The GPS says Disneyland is an hour and fifteen minutes away, although at the speed I'm going, we'll probably get there sooner. I'm driving too fast, but it feels too good to slow down.

I learned how to drive when I was fourteen. It's the one thing Jack taught me. We had just arrived at the house in Amagansett for the last few weeks of summer. It was our first morning there, and Louisa asked Jack to go into town for some coffee and croissants from the farmers' market. "Why doesn't Amos join you?" she said in a way that was more of a demand than a suggestion. I didn't care enough to object, so I followed Jack out the door. As we walked down the gravel driveway to his 1978 Mercedes SL, he tossed me the keys. "You're up," he said. I looked at him, confused.

"Quick, before your mom sees."

As I got behind the wheel and buckled up, Jack told me he wasn't going to have me be one of those sissy Manhattan schoolboys who didn't know how to drive. I put the key into the ignition, my hands shaking. Jack loved his Benz. But he seemed confident that I wouldn't crash his car or kill us both.

"There's nothing more dangerous on the road than fear," he said. I nodded, trying my best not to look as afraid as I felt.

I slowly turned the key, and jumped from the roar of the engine. It reverberated in every bone in my body. I put the car in drive and slowly tapped on the gas. We jolted forward, and I slammed on the brake. Jack just laughed.

"Let yourself feel the car," he said. I nodded, and cursed myself for being such a wuss. I adjusted the mirror again. I ran my fingers along the steering wheel, feeling the smooth leather under my skin. Again I lifted my foot off the brake, but this time I placed it on the gas and pushed on it gently. The engine purred, and man, it felt good. We glided forward, and I pressed down on the gas harder. We drove a couple of loops around the property until I started to get the hang of it. Finally, he gave me the go-ahead to turn onto Main Street. I had never felt power like this before. I pushed down on the gas even more.

"Whoa, now," Jack said. "Let's not get ourselves pulled over."

Just a mile down the road, at the glorified farm stand, Jack ordered two espressos to go, and handed one to me on our way out. I took a sip of the drink, and even though it was painfully bitter, it tasted exactly like being an adult.

Jack and my mom had been married for seven years, but he and I had never spent much time alone together. We weren't exactly going to throw a football around in the park on a spring day. But for the rest of that summer, Jack would offer to run random errands for Louisa, and I'd nonchalantly agree to tag along. The drives became our thing. And it was weird, because for the first time, I found myself wanting Jack to like me.

When Flynn arrived a few months later, I thought it meant that Jack would be around the apartment more, but somehow he was around even less.

"Amos, you're going kind of fast," Flynn says. I hear the faint sound of police sirens in the distance, and slow down. But the wailing gets louder and louder, and I see a police car approaching in my rearview mirror.

"Uh-oh," Flynn mutters as she looks back over her shoulder.

"You don't think Neel called the cops on us, do you?" I ask her.

"No," she responds. And then, more dubiously: "I don't know."

"Just tell them there's been a misunderstanding," Poppy suggests. "That's what they say when things like this happen on TV." The kid's got a point.

The sirens are getting closer. "Just let me do the talking, okay?" The girls nod. I signal, and look over my shoulder, as I start to pull over to the side of the road. The cop car is right behind us now. I take a deep breath, steadying myself. But then . . . the car zooms right past us. We all look at each other, confused and elated, and so completely relieved.

"I guess things can always be worse," Poppy says. And then we just start laughing—at ourselves, at the ridiculousness of this whole scenario. Flynn messes with the radio and settles on some pop song. It's catchy and annoying, and I hate that I know the words to it. Flynn sings along, and soon Poppy does, too. Flynn looks at me with a slight smile. We both seem to have surrendered ourselves to a sense of temporary calm, which I'm grateful for. And so I smile back at her, turn up the volume, and join in.

POPPY

We're here! We're here! Dear Neel Khan, thank you for letting us borrow your car and credit card. Well, I guess we didn't borrow them, because he didn't actually offer them to us. But if there is a God, and I'm not totally sure there is, I think he would understand that right now we have to bend the rules a little. I hate breaking rules, but I think it's okay. At least, I hope it is.

Luckily, just as I'm starting to "spiral," as Susan calls it, Amos turns to me. "Ready, Fred?" he asks. Sometimes we call each other Fred. Like "ready Freddy." He holds up three giant passes, waving them around like we've found the golden tickets. Flynn and I fly over to him, and then we're off!

We pass through the big gates, and I'm so excited I can barely breathe. Main Street, U.S.A., is everything I hoped it would be and more—it's like I've stepped into *Meet Me in St. Louis* or something. But better. And because it's Christmas, there are Mickey-shaped decorations, and twinkle lights sparkle on a giant tree. Did you know Main Street is actually based on the town Walt Disney himself grew up in? I read that in one of my books. The buildings here all look like they're from the 1900s—with colorful awnings and quaint little storefronts. There's an opera house, and a cinema and a redbrick fire station. Everything looks simple—nothing like the massiveness of Manhattan. Four men ride by on one bicycle and wave. They're in different-colored pin-striped suits, and singing in perfect harmony.

I can't help but laugh a little to myself at what my mom would think. Disneyland is pretty much everything in life that she hates. To start with, she is afraid of fried food. I'm not even joking. Like, she's actually scared of it. One time, when her sister (who I don't think she likes very much) was visiting us in New York, she ordered beignets for dessert. When Aunt Mimi got up to go to the bathroom, I heard Mom say, "She should just stick them on her ass and save them the trip."

The other reason my mom would hate Disneyland is that she hates standing in lines. That lady won't stand in line for anything. I think that's why she always says she "loathes amusement parks," and probably why I never get to go to any. That and all "the people." The way she says *people,* it's like they're something sticky and disgusting, and contagious. No, my mom would not like Disneyland at all. Too many people, waiting in too many lines, wearing too many tank tops. Tank tops are another one of my mom's pet peeves. She's seriously offended by that little flap of fat right by your armpit. She strongly believes that arms, like toes, should be covered in public at all times. Even on beach vacations!

My mom is funny like that. She has a lot of things she "firmly believes." I guess you could say she has a lot of opinions. Like, she doesn't believe in bottles on the table, or the word *sucks,* or the color pink at all. Ever. Like, anywhere. And we're never allowed to watch TV and eat at the same time, except on Sundays, and only if it's raining. When it comes down to it, I guess she's really kind of snobby sometimes. Like, I'm sure she was totally a Tatiana when she was in elementary school. If she was in my class, I don't think I would like her very much.

"Where to first?" Amos asks.

"Good question," I say, and take out our map. "Well, I think we obviously have to start in Fantasyland."

"Naturally," Amos teases.

I study the layout of the park closely—we've got to be smart about this. "First maybe Peter Pan's Flight, then Mr. Toad's Wild Ride, the tea cups, Alice, and of course It's a Small World. Then we can make it to some of the real rides like Big Thunder Mountain and Splash Mountain before it gets too crowded. I'm fine skipping the Jungle Cruise, but if we hurry, we can make it to the Haunted Mansion before lunch. . . . Oh! And then Toontown and Tomorrowland, too. Sound good?"

"You're the boss, Boss," he answers.

This really is the Happiest Place on Earth!

63

AMOS

We make our way down Main Street, and the air is full of butter and sugar and ragtime music. The sweet smells are no doubt emanating from one of the countless eateries, which are all called cutesy things like the Jolly Holiday Bakery and the Refreshment Corner. And a cast member is playing cheerful tunes on a small red-and-white piano to entertain the park visitors as they enjoy their snacks on an outdoor patio. We pause for a minute to listen. When the pianist finishes, a few onlookers clap politely. The pianist, clad in a red-and-white-striped three-piece suit, invites anyone who wants to take a turn at the keyboard. A young mother attempts to persuade her little boy to give it a try, but he refuses—hiding himself between his mom's legs. I look at Flynn.

"I dare you," I challenge her. And she looks at me like I'm certifiably nuts.

"Flynn hasn't been playing piano lately," Poppy explains.

"Well, that's a damn shame," I say, nudging Flynn forward. "C'mon, we want to hear you!"

"Yeah! C'mon!" Poppy's revved up.

She shakes her head and starts to walk away. "Do it, do it!" Poppy and I goad. And soon, others around us are joining in. The piano player steps aside to make room for her. But Flynn's not budging. The chanting gets louder, and suddenly, *not* doing it is drawing more attention to Flynn than just getting it over with. Poppy gently pushes her toward the podium. She turns back and shoots me a look.

"I hate you right now," she says with a smirk, and she reluctantly makes her way to the piano and shyly takes a seat.

"Ohmygosh!" Poppy says giddily.

What should I play? I can see Flynn mouth to herself. Her fingers dance nervously above the keys. She closes her eyes and takes a deep breath. And then the notes start, tentatively at first. She looks over at Poppy and me, and we offer an encouraging thumbs-up. The song starts to gain momentum as her fingers look like they're almost flying over the keys.

"My favorite!" Poppy exclaims. Soon, a twinkle of recognition spreads among the small crowd as Flynn's rendition of "Let It Go" gets louder. And then, to my surprise, Poppy spontaneously starts to sing. And one by one, the people around us join in for a *Frozen* sing-along. More and more people gather, and soon everyone is belting out the words—even me. The song ends, and everyone applauds. Flynn smiles brightly, and Poppy and I are ecstatic. I knew she could do it.

64

FLYNN

Leave it to Walt Disney to cure a case of stage fright. But deep down, I know it hasn't strictly been performance anxiety that's kept me from the piano for the past few months. I can't explain it, but somehow when Amos left, I had this strange realization. I was tired of having people and things taken away from me. It's like I subconsciously decided that I would renounce everything that mattered to me before that could happen again. Maybe it's some twisted form of control or something? But trying to control everything all the time is exhausting, and I'm tired of fighting it. Like the song says, maybe it is time to "let it go." All of it. It felt amazing to play again.

I look around the park—it's weird to be back here. When I was a kid, way back when I had two living parents who were actually married to each other, my mom and dad took me to Disneyland. I think I must have been about four at the time. Weirdly, I remember being more excited about the drive down the coast than I was about our big Disney adventure. It felt so thrilling to wake up when it was still dark out, pack up the Jeep with snacks and CDs, and head out on the road.

I remember we stopped at In-N-Out and all got burgers and vanilla milk shakes. Even then, something about the whole trip felt so precious, almost ephemeral, like somehow I knew that none of it would last. Like I had some uncanny premonition that that brief weekend trip would be the only one I'd remember with my family. My first family.

I only have two real memories of Disneyland. The first is of all the people. It was Labor Day, so there were tourists everywhere. Even though I tried to hold on to my dad's hand, the force of the crowd pulled us apart. I remember panicking as I searched the sea of legs, before finding my dad's sneakers. I grabbed his thigh, only to realize that the man looking down at me was not my father at all. Just some guy with indistinguishable denim and what looked to me to be identical sneakers. Before my startle could turn to tears, my dad reached down and swept me up onto his shoulders. From that perch, I could see Sleeping Beauty's castle in the distance. I was young enough then to believe that a real princess lived up in that tower. I was young enough then to believe in happily ever after.

The only other memory I have from the trip I'm not even sure if I truly remember, or if I invented it from a photograph that was always on our old piano. It was of my mom and me on the tea cups. I'm wearing my favorite purple dress and turquoise cardigan, and I have a giant grin on my face. My mom is next to me, her hair blowing in the wind as we spin around and around. She has me wrapped in her long elegant arms—she's so beautiful, and I'm so safe beside her.

Now, all these years later, I walk down Main Street, U.S.A., with Amos and Poppy, and I feel like a totally different person. I spot Donald, Mickey, and Pluto and watch as little kids rush over, burrowing themselves into their soft plush coats. For a second, I wish I weren't old enough to know that it's not really Pluto. Probably just some perv in a dog suit. But still, the pure elation on those little kids' faces is enviable. Part of me wishes I were that innocent again. I guess I wish a lot of things. But for now, with Poppy as our fearless leader, we march through Sleeping Beauty's castle and disappear into Fantasyland.

AMOS

"Let's go!" Poppy exclaims, and she takes my hand and charges ahead. I grab Flynn's so I don't lose her in the crowd. I forgot how delicate her hands are. We're practically running through the castle—our adrenaline and excitement propelling us forward. We've been running for three days straight now, and I wonder when we'll run out of steam.

Per Poppy's directions, we head to Peter Pan's Flight first, and slowly snake our way to the front of the line. The three of us climb into a ship. "Come on, everybody! Here we go!" Peter welcomes us, and we fly out of the nursery window to embark on an adventure, just like the children in the story. I've always loved this one. A world full of pirates, and Lost Boys, and Never Land. Life back at our West Village apartment sometimes felt like Never Land—Clay certainly wasn't going to grow up, and when he was in charge, I was allowed to build forts, and jump on beds, and live in whatever fantasy I could dream up.

It's weird to think that Clay finally grew up. And sobered up. And that I didn't give him—my own father—the benefit of the doubt. What if we hadn't come to LA? Would I have just gone on thinking he was having beer for breakfast when all the while he was doing yoga, and making juice, and hoping that one day I would call him back?

It's ironic—I thought that the only thing I wanted was to grow up. That if I left my childhood home, I'd be leaving childhood, too, and maybe things on the other side would make more sense. But I've actually been doing the total opposite. I've been running away from growing up altogether.

Flynn requests the tea cups next. We all settle into a giant turquoise cup, and the girls put me in charge of spinning the wheel. We turn around and around—Poppy and Flynn holding on to each other tightly—until we all start turning green. We're wobbly when we exit, and it takes us a minute to find our footing. If only real life worked like that: just as things started to spin out of control, you could take your hands off the wheel, and everything could be just as it was.

"What's next?" I ask Poppy.

"How about something a little more . . ." Her body sways from side to side.

"Stationary?" I suggest.

"Small World!" she cries. We make our way over to the gleaming white-and-gold ride, and groan at the sight of the insanely long line extending past the designated barriers. There's a mob of Japanese tourists in front of us in matching polo shirts and visors.

"Let's come back later," I say.

"No," Poppy protests. "It's the ride I want to go on the most." I know she means it. When Poppy was in kindergarten, her class performed the song during her school's holiday recital. She drove Rosie and me crazy for months after, still singing that freaking song all over the apartment.

"C'mon. We don't want to waste all day waiting in line. Let's hit up the Haunted Mansion, get some lunch, and we'll come back later."

"But what if there's not time?" Poppy says, digging her heels into the ground.

"We'll make sure there's time. We'll come back on the way out," Flynn assures her.

"Promise?" she asks. Her voice wavers; she's on the brink of tears.

"Promise," Flynn replies.

We pinky-swear that we'll come back before we leave the park, and Poppy seems satisfied with the compromise. She links one arm with Flynn's, and the other with mine, and we set off for our next adventure.

66

FLYNN

Since we've got Neel's credit card, we decide to splurge and avoid the long lines at the myriad of fried food places, and instead eat at the Blue Bayou in New Orleans Square. Entering the restaurant, we step out of the bright high-noon light and into the murky darkness of a French Quarter night. Even though we're technically inside, they've created the illusion of evening with a night-sky projection, hanging lights, sound effects, and even glowing fireflies. We sit down, and it feels good to be off my feet for a moment. Despite the Pirates of the Caribbean ride sailing by us, the dim lighting provides a respite from the sensory overload outside, and I realize I'm actually starving.

Problem is, when the food comes it is still barely edible theme-park fare. Poppy ordered pasta from the kids' menu, and it's the only thing that looks mildly appealing, so she invites Amos and me to share.

"I'm not hungry," she says, which is weird. Maybe she's still shaken up from the Haunted Mansion? I could see how that kind of thing wouldn't be her speed, but she seemed so excited to go. I want to cheer her up, so I tear the paper off one end of my straw and blow through it, sending the remaining paper flying at her. She barely cracks a smile.

"Poppy, what's wrong? Are you okay?" I ask.

"Nothing. I'm fine," she mumbles, but I'm not sure I'm buying it.

Amos and I steal a quick look at each other. He senses she's not herself, too. Amos sticks his fork into her spaghetti, takes a long strand, and then lets it dangle from his mouth. She seems unamused. Distant. I try something else.

"Who am I?" I challenge her as I take the other side of Amos's spaghetti strand, just like in *Lady and the Tramp.* She can't help but crack a smile. Then, to her delight, I slurp up the spaghetti until Amos's and my mouths nearly meet. His lips are so close to mine, and there is only this awkward piece of pasta between us. I find myself wanting to erase the stupid noodle, and the fake frog sounds from the restaurant, and even Poppy's watchful eyes. For a moment, I want all the distance between us gone. I want to feel Amos's face near mine, to remember the taste of his tongue. I want it to happen all over again.

"Do it again! Do it again!" Poppy goads us on.

But the noodle breaks, and the moment has passed.

67

POPPY

There's no turning back now. We're locked in, and lined up single file in a log—Flynn's in front, then me, then Amos. I'm trying not to think about the FIFTY-FOOT PLUNGE AHEAD sign. I'm trying not to think about the queasy feeling taking over my insides. I'm trying to think, *This is fun!* A voice says, "Have a zip-a-dee-doo-dah ride!" as we start the climb up Splash Mountain.

"You okay?" Flynn calls back to me.

"You're sure I'm not going to fall out?" I ask, my voice shaking with fear and excitement.

"I promise," she says. "Just hold on tight." Of course, she and my brother told me that we didn't have to go on something so scary, that we could start off with some of the smaller rides first. But I know they think the Haunted Mansion really freaked me out, so I want to show them I can do the big kid stuff, too.

We start off with a small dip. My stomach drops, and I let out a yelp. Now we're cruising through the tunnel with old-timey singing frogs, foxes, birds, and rabbits, and I'm not sure if they're supposed to be cute or creepy. Suddenly it feels like we've been in the darkness for way too long. Which only means one thing. It's coming. The big one.

We start to go way up, the wheels creaking loudly. I tell myself it's just a sound effect. We're getting closer to the top and closer and closer and closer and I'm holding my breath and then . . . down we go! I scream so loud, and it feels so good and scary and awful and amazing. We land in the pool at the bottom, and water splashes everywhere. I'm drenched from head to toe, and as I wipe my eyes, my cheeks hurt from smiling so hard.

68

AMOS

Flynn and I sit on a bench in the sun to dry off outside Splash Mountain, while Poppy evaluates the photo board to see if they got a good shot of us free-falling.

"Second wife," Flynn says. It takes me a minute to notice the awkwardly mismatched couple getting handsy by the hot-dog cart.

"He used to be fat, but recently got rich and lost a ton of weight," I hypothesize in regard to the man in mom jeans and a fanny pack.

"Surgically," she notes.

"Is there any other way?" I joke.

"He ditched his first wife for the girl who wouldn't give him the time of day in high school. They reconnected on Facebook," Flynn adds.

"She was going to be a star. But she peaked at her senior prom," I continue, eyeing the woman with teased hair and wearing cutoffs with the bottom half of her ass hanging out.

"Back home he has a room of collectible Disney figurines, and she has a princess complex."

"Totally," I laugh.

"And so here we are on their honeymoon," she continues.

She nailed it, as always. We chuckle to ourselves. "So . . . Clay's sober," I say, and it feels good to finally tell her.

"Wow, that's . . ." Flynn looks at me and takes it in. She always held out hope that Clay could clean up his act one day—even when I didn't.

"Yeah."

"How are you feeling about it?" she asks.

"Good. I think. It's strange, because on the one hand, I feel like he's back, and on the other, it's like I don't even know him at all." I change the subject. "So are we just not going to talk about you and the piano?"

"We don't have to. . . ." She looks at me, her expression serious. "But thank you. It felt good to be back in the saddle again."

"Yeah, well, you looked good up there." We hold each other's gaze, like we're both about to say something.

But then Poppy comes barreling back from the picture board. "Our eyes were closed in all of them!"

"That's okay—we'll get another shot of us later," Flynn reassures her. And the moment between us has passed. "I don't know about you guys, but I could use some dry clothes."

The sun felt good, but my shirt is still damp. "How about a wardrobe change?" I suggest, and then follow the girls as they race into the Westward Ho Trading Company.

69

FLYNN

We pick out a Donald Duck sweatshirt for Amos, Ariel for Poppy, and Simba for me, and Mickey Mouse ears all around. May as well go all out. "Thanks, Neel. You can add it to the tab," I say, as I hand over his credit card to pay for our souvenirs up at the register.

We throw on our new gear (mouse ears and all), and Poppy insists on taking a selfie. As we wait for the Polaroid to develop, I'm hit with a pang of sadness. Because this really is all coming to an end—not just our adventure here in LA, but Amos, Poppy, and me. Whatever we are will no longer be. I spent so many nights, when I first got to New York, wishing I were back in California. But now, Woodside doesn't feel like home anymore.

I look at the picture as it slowly comes into view—our happy faces crammed together, Poppy in the middle, Amos and me barely in the frame. Poppy and Amos have always looked more like actual siblings—they both have Louisa's fair skin and wide-set blue eyes. But Poppy and I have the same goofy grin, and somehow I feel better knowing we'll always share that.

"What's next?" Amos asks as I follow him out of the store. And because this is it, because this is the end, I take his hand in mine.

"You choose."

AMOS

Flynn takes my hand, and it brings an involuntary smile to my face. I feel caught. She has this way of stripping away the façade. It's nothing calculated on her part. Nothing she's even aware of. But when she looks at me like that—straight on—she destroys me all over again.

My choice. "Tomorrowland. It's the only place we have left to go." And I smile because it's true—our family, our lives as we knew them are already a thing of the past. One way or another we'll have to move forward. We'll go back home, even though everything will be different. Like Tomorrowland, it will be a future full of nostalgia. I sense myself becoming morose, but I feel an obligation to make the best of what's left of today. I pocket Poppy's Polaroid in the wallet Jack got me last Christmas, and put my arm around Flynn.

"Shall we?" I ask her.

She wraps her long arm around me, hooking her finger on

one of the belt loops of my jeans. It feels intimate, and I like it. The proximity. We let ourselves walk like this—holding each other. Flynn smiles, and I see she's distracted watching our feet. She's trying to sync our steps. I try to throw her off. It's stupid. It's a thing we used to do. We're so focused, looking down, that we plow into a group of kids and nearly trip over ourselves.

I jokingly give her a shove and look back at Poppy. "Psyched for Space Mountain?"

Only Poppy is not behind me.

"Poppy?" I call out.

"What's wrong?" Flynn asks, turning around.

"Where is she?" I yell back, not meaning for it to be *at* her.

"I don't know . . . she was right here."

"Well, clearly she's not."

"Poppy!" Flynn shouts frantically.

Our eyes scan the crowd of khaki shorts and chubby legs, sunburns, sandals, and strollers for any sign of our little sister. I don't see her anywhere.

"Shit, Amos! What do we do?" Flynn asks, as if I have any freaking clue.

"Retrace our steps. She couldn't have gone far," I say in a way that I hope masks my anxiety.

I'm mad. But not at Flynn. I should have known better. I can't let the world fall apart every time she looks at me. That's what got us here in the first place.

71

POPPY

Where's my camera? I need my camera. My eyes search everywhere.

"Excuse me?" a lady scolds me as we collide, but I don't have any time to stop and say sorry. I don't see it anywhere. But it has to be somewhere. My camera! How could I lose it? It's my most important possession. I swear I had it around my neck a few seconds ago in the gift shop. Did I leave it there? I must have left it there. Maybe it's by the register? Or over by the sweatshirts? I've gotta get my camera.

FLYNN

"Poppy!" I call out as I sprint back in the direction of the gift shop. Amos runs up to random strangers, asking if they've seen our little sister, but no one is of any help. How is this happening? Where could she be? She was right behind us.

"How do you keep losing her?" Amos yells at me as we scour the herds of people outside the store.

Seriously? Isn't it just like him to blame me. I'm not even going to dignify that with a response. I ignore him. Where is she? I need to keep moving.

"Good, Flynn. Not talking to me is really going to help the situation right now," Amos rants.

I can't take it anymore. I whip around. "How is it possible for you to never take any responsibility for anything?" I yell at him.

"I'm the irresponsible one?" Amos snaps.

"Why don't you just let me deal with this—like everything else?"

"Like how you dealt with last night?"

That was low. I charge ahead, calling Poppy's name and moving so fast through the crowds that Amos can barely keep up.

"Flynn! Slow down! Stop running!" he calls after me. But I can't. I don't slow down, and I don't turn back. Because we have to find her. We just *have* to find her.

73

AMOS

"Are you kidding me right now?" I finally catch up to Flynn. I grab her arm to try to get her to stop for a minute.

"Amos, I'm not gonna waste time fighting with you." She doesn't look at me, her eyes darting in a million different directions. "Do you think she went to find a bathroom? Or maybe she got ahead of us and she's already at Space Mountain? What if someone took her?"

"We'll look everywhere—we'll find her," I say.

"This place is massive. She could be anywhere. We need to split up."

"So that you and I lose each other, too? No way."

"We never should have tossed our phones. That was so dumb," Flynn laments.

"Well, that's not really helpful now, is it?" I fire back. "We never should have done a lot of things."

She flinches and swallows hard. She looks at the clock on Sleeping Beauty's castle. "Meet back here in forty-five minutes. At three o'clock."

And then we race off, in a desperate search to find our sister.

POPPY

My camera isn't inside the store. I ask the woman at the register if she's seen it. She says no and tells me to go to Lost and Found. Lost and Found? Come on, lady. She must have spent too long in Fantasyland. If someone finds a camera, they're going to keep it. It's gone. My camera is gone forever.

One . . . two . . . I'm trying to count, trying to calm down, but I'm too dizzy and light-headed. One . . . two . . . I can't get to three. There isn't enough air in here. I have to get outside. I push my way out of the store and look around for Flynn and Amos. But I don't see them. We were all together. But then . . . my camera.

I climb onto a bench and nudge a mother and her toddler out of the way so I can stand up to see better. I look everywhere. It feels like that game you play when you're little: I spy. I spy with my little eye . . . you know? But I don't spy Amos or Flynn anywhere. In fact, nothing here looks familiar, and now I'm wondering if I went out a different exit than before. Maybe I should go back in the store? Or maybe I should wait here in case they come looking for me? Maybe I should go to the Disneyland police, but I don't want Flynn and Amos to get mad at me for turning us in.

I decide to keep walking because I don't know what else to do.

"Flynn! Amos!" I cry out, but they're not anywhere. I wasn't in the store for that long. Was I? Did they just forget about me? Maybe they don't even realize I'm gone. Amos said he wanted to go on Space Mountain next. I bet they're there. That must be it. I just have to get to Tomorrowland.

I'm trying to figure out which way to go, but there's a baby crying its head off, and a group of carolers singing "Santa Claus Is Coming to Town," so it's really hard to think. They are smiling at me with these creepy grins, and they're way too loud. I walk away, but I get trampled by a herd of teenage boys running past me. I fall to the ground. My hands burn from hitting the pavement, and I feel tears streaming down my cheeks. I need Flynn and Amos. Where are they? What if no one finds me? I've wanted to come to Disneyland my whole entire life, and now all I want to do is go home. But what if I never get there?

75

FLYNN

She isn't in the store, or in line again at Splash Mountain. She isn't back by the churro stand. Or at Space Mountain. I run frantically through the park, suddenly glad for all the training I've been doing. I'm trying to be fast, but also alert enough to not miss her. I feel like I'm in one of those *Where's Waldo?* books. Everybody looks like Poppy but isn't Poppy. All the while I know that this search is probably futile. She's probably looking for us, too. We're bound to run in circles—destined to keep missing each other.

We're so dumb. Poppy has the tendency to run off. We know this. We should have made a plan—if one of us gets lost, we meet back at X. Defeated, I start to make my way to Sleeping Beauty's castle. The big hand on the giant clock creeps toward the twelve, and I'm full of dread.

I let myself believe for a second that Amos found her. That she's safe and sound. I anticipate how it will feel to see them in the periphery and then watch them round the corner together and walk toward me. I imagine throwing my arms around Poppy. I would apologize to her. For everything. And I would tell her that she's my sister—my whole sister—and that I will love her for always. The thought makes me giddy, but then I spot Amos in the distance . . . and he's alone.

I crumple down to the curb. Amos hovers over me. And now I'm angry. At Poppy for wandering off. At Amos for everything. But mostly I'm angry at myself. This was my idea. All of it. I look up at Amos and squint into the sun as I say to him, "We really fucked up."

"Come on," Amos says, taking my hand and pulling me up.

"Where are we going?" I ask.

"To get help."

76

AMOS

Flynn and I run up to a portly dude barely older than I am, a little too eager to wear his Disneyland security badge, if you know what I mean. Not so surprisingly, he tells us that kids get lost here all the time. He takes us to the Baby Center, basically the park's Lost and Found for kids. But there is no sign of her. Then we follow the guy to City Hall, where he asks us to explain exactly how we lost our little sister. He asks to see a picture of Poppy, and we have to tell them that we don't have one.

"You don't have a picture of your sister anywhere on your phone?" he inquires dubiously.

"I don't have my phone on me," I reply.

"And what about you?" He turns his questioning toward Flynn. "You must have a picture of your sister somewhere on yours. Facebook? Instagram? Anything?"

"I don't have my phone, either," Flynn answers sheepishly.

And now Tweedledum is downright suspicious.

"So you're telling me that neither of you two teenagers have a cell phone on your person?"

Flynn and I shake our heads, looking undoubtedly suspect. Part of me feels like we should just come clean and tell him everything. Especially when he starts asking about our parents. Of course he wants to talk to Jack and Louisa, but they're not supposed to land in LA for a few hours. They were mad enough when I spoke to them this morning—I can't even imagine how they will react to this. Not like we don't deserve it.

"Oh, wait!" I say, remembering the Polaroid in my wallet. "It's blurry, but that's her in the middle." The guy takes the photo from me.

"All right, sit tight. Any information we get is going to come through here first. If it's any consolation, we've never not found a child. In the meantime, is there an adult you kids can call?" he asks, although it sounds more like an accusation.

I'm this close to breaking down, to just pouring my heart out and explaining to him that, no, there really isn't anyone else for us to call. We're all we've got. But there's something tugging inside me, because I know, of course, that there is one call I could make.

POPPY

It's a world of laughter, a world of tears. It's a world of hope and a world of fears. The song won't stop playing in my head on repeat as I try to make my way through the crowds in search of my older siblings. But I'm only fifty-four inches tall, and I feel like I'm being tossed around in a sea of grown-ups, and toddlers and backpacks, and strollers. There's a holiday parade passing, with nutcrackers marching and women dressed as snowflakes roller-skating by. Mickey and Minnie wave from a float as it starts to snow from I don't know where. I try to ride the wave, but now I can't tell if I'm going backward or forward, or just around and around in circles. Like when I had an anxiety attack on the Central Park Carousel. Round and round and round. I have to get off. It has to stop. Make it stop. Where are Flynn and Amos? *It's a world of laughter, a world of tears. It's a world of hope and a world of fears.* Someone make it stop.

I put my hands over my ears, but the song continues in my head anyway. *It's a world of laughter, a world of tears. It's a world of hope and a world of fears.* I realize that I'm sobbing, and when I do, it scares me. I want to scream, but I don't even think anyone would hear me. I need to get away from this parade. The tears are pouring out so fast, it's hard to see. Like that time we had to pull over on the Long Island Expressway because the rain was coming down faster than the windshield wipers could wipe. I can't see where I'm going. But then suddenly, through the blur, I see a flash of color. And then I feel a hand on my shoulder. It's Flynn! Finally. But as the face comes into view, I see it's not Flynn at all. It's Snow White.

78

FLYNN

"We're going to find her," I say, attempting to reassure Amos.

"I know," he says, sounding anything but certain.

And we go back to sitting in silence on the steps outside City Hall. Both, I'm sure, imagining the worst. I pick at something purplish and sticky on my jeans. I wish we'd never run. I wasn't thinking. I was being reckless. And now we're sitting here without our little sister. How could I have been so careless?

I pick harder at the purplish gunk as I try to fight back the tears that are starting to feel unavoidable. But the only thing it accomplishes is that I now have the suspicious substance stuck under my fingernails, too. No wonder Louisa hates amusement parks. Despite the incessant blasting of cheery music, glisten of fresh paint, and perfectly trimmed topiaries, this place is absolutely filthy. And just like that, I can't keep it in any longer. A single tear escapes, and I try to surreptitiously wipe it away, so I don't alarm Amos any more.

"We're going to find her," Amos says, taking his turn to try to calm us.

I'm afraid I'll sob if I try to speak, and anyway, I'm not sure I agree with him, so instead I simply keep my head down, and nod.

Every second that we wait feels elongated with all the inevitabilities. *This is it,* I think. *This is how you end up on the morning news.* I imagine us on the *Today* show, making a tear-filled plea to Savannah as she feigns sympathy for our lost little sister. We'll show a picture of Poppy—but which one? Then, out of nowhere, I laugh out loud. Amos looks at me questioningly.

"Remember that time we lost Poppy at Aunt Mimi's wedding?" I say to him.

"How could I forget?"

Poppy was only about two at the time. We were all in Miami for Louisa's crazy younger sister's first wedding. "Halfway through the trip, the nanny quit with no notice. What was her name again?" I ask Amos.

"Stella?"

"Della!" It's all coming back to me now.

"Of course. Good ol' Della—that poor woman. Smarter than she seemed. She got out when she could."

"She always ate that vile spread."

"Vegemite! I used to have nightmares about that shit."

"Ugh, if I close my eyes I can still smell it. Disgusting."

Anyway, Della up and abandoned us (and really, who could blame her). So, naturally, Jack and Louisa had a panic attack at the prospect of being stuck on vacation alone with their three small children, and they immediately employed the hotel to find some local lady to look after us.

We were all part of the bridal party. Amos and I already felt like old pros on the wedding circuit, having attended Jack and Louisa's a few years back. After the ceremony we were allowed to linger at cocktail hour. But as soon as the doors opened, and the guests were escorted into the grand ballroom, we kids were whisked away—it was always the intent that we'd disappear during the dinner and dancing that followed. So here's this poor local babysitter, stuck shuttling three unwilling kids up to bed in the elevator. She hit the button for the top floor, and Amos and I continued to complain about missing all the fun. The elevator stopped to let some other passengers off on a lower floor. They made their exit, relieved to be free of the whiny children, no doubt. And just as the doors were nearly closed, with an opening only big enough for a two-year-old to sneak through, Poppy made her escape!

The problem was, of course, that none of us were paying close enough attention to know which floor we had just stopped on. Amos and I were in knots—uncontrollably giggling at the audacity of our littlest sibling. It was, as far as we were concerned, Poppy's first act of independence. I think unconsciously we were both a bit inspired by the defiant little personality that was emerging. But needless to say, this poor babysitter was beside herself. Though she wasn't the sharpest tool in the shed, even she must have foreseen the disappearance of her big payday with the disappearance of her smallest charge. She had an immediate meltdown and started praying to Jesus.

It was Amos who had the bright idea of alerting the hotel authorities. While the three of us ran up and down the hallways, screaming Poppy's name, with a doorman who in retrospect was no more than twenty-two and most definitely on drugs, hotel security scoured the surveillance footage for any sign of our two-and-a-half-foot-tall little sister. For Amos and me, it was all a hysterical adventure. We were small enough not to worry about all the dangers that could befall her. She could have made her way up to the roof, or out the front door and into traffic, or God forbid into the arms of any one of the bad people that we know now to be afraid of. Only years later does it seem strange that no one thought to get our parents out of the party to tell them about the situation.

When we finally found Poppy, it turned out she had found her way into the arms of the housekeeping staff, who'd deposited her at the hotel's front desk. She was sitting with the concierge, so content, and so oblivious to all the chaos she had created.

"We're going to find her," I say again. And this time, I believe it.

AMOS

I'm starting to lose my mind, sitting here. Waiting. Flynn pulls a pack of Sour Patch Kids from her backpack and offers it to me. I pour some of the sugary candies out and hand Flynn the green ones, because I know they're her favorite.

"Thanks," she says.

And then we continue to sit. And wait. I look over at Flynn, who's twirling the short strands of her hair.

"Flynn, I'm sorry," I offer, my voice tired and penitent.

She shakes her head. "It's both of our faults. We should have kept a better eye on her. We got distracted and—"

"No, I mean, not just about Poppy." I take a deep breath. "About . . . everything."

She keeps her eyes fixed to the floor. "Amos, it's fine. I get it. You didn't want to be around me anymore, so you left, and—"

"Wait, is that what you really think? Flynn, that's not it at all. What happened between us was . . ."

"Confusing?"

"Yeah. And scary. But also not scary. Because it's you. And everything with you always feels good. And right. But I was so afraid that I would scare you, or hurt you, or ruin us, and . . . and so I did nothing."

"You didn't do nothing, Amos. You left."

"I didn't know what else to do. I kept thinking I would suddenly know what to say to you, or understand how I was feeling. But June turned into September, and then it was December, and . . ."

"Here we are."

We sit, not saying anything. Finally, she looks at me. "You know, it's really messed up. That you would just leave like that," she says. "You think I wasn't confused? Or hurt? Or afraid? And I was just left there. To sit with your silence."

"I'm sorry. I really am," I say, wishing there were a bigger word for sorry.

"Well, now that we're here . . . what are you thinking?" she asks me.

"That I care about you more than I ever thought I could care about anyone. But also that—"

"We can't be together." She finishes my thought.

"At least not right now," I add. "It's too . . ."

"Complicated?" Flynn suggests.

"Just with everything—with our parents. Life feels too messy right now. I don't want what's happening with us to get mixed up in their bullshit."

She nods, as if she's processing.

"What are *you* thinking?" I return the question.

"I think you're right," she says after a moment. "Our family's in free fall, and we have no idea where we're going to land. I've lost so much. . . . I can't risk losing you, too." She pauses, and then adds, "I need to know we'll always be friends. Well, not friends, but . . ."

"Us," I say. She smiles.

"But, Flynn, what's been going on with you lately? Your hair? The piercing? And don't even get me started on that toolbox Neel Khan."

She playfully nudges me. "He's not that bad. I don't know . . . it was never really about him anyway. I think—I think I just needed to feel like someone other than myself for a little," she says. And then after a while she adds, "And I missed you."

"I missed you, too."

She nods. "How do we go back to the place where we can just be you and me?"

"Amos!" a voice calls out, saving me from having to figure out the answer. Believe me, turning to him for help was the last thing I wanted to do. I wasn't even sure he'd pick up the phone when I called—let alone show up. And yet here he is. We both stand up.

"Flynn, this is my dad, Clay."

Flynn takes him in. "It's nice to meet you." She looks at me. "I'm . . . going to check back in," she says, and goes inside. And I know that she's doing it as much out of concern for Poppy as she is to give me a few minutes alone with Clay.

"Your mom's a nervous wreck," he offers once we're alone.

"You've been talking to Louisa?" I ask him, genuinely

shocked that the two of them could be conspiring about anything together.

"You think I didn't realize something was going on when you just showed up at my door?" I guess I'm more cynical than I thought, because I honestly didn't think Clay would care enough to try to connect the dots. "Come on, kid. Give me a little more credit than that."

"I'm just surprised. I didn't think you'd jump at the opportunity to communicate with my mom. Last I checked, you two were still persona non grata with each other."

"Well, sometimes we do things we really don't want to do for the people we love."

"Yeah," I say, looking down. I know he's sincere; I just don't know how to take it. I'm not used to hearing him talk this way, and it's making me uncomfortable. "Well, thanks, I guess."

We sit back down on the steps and just kind of stare at the ground.

"Listen, kid," Clay says, "I know there's no way to say sorry to you for the things I've done, and all the ways I haven't been there for you over the years." He puts his hand on my back. "But I want to be in your life."

"What is this, some kind of amends?" I ask, slipping into a petulant tone I don't mean to use.

"Would it be okay with you if it was?"

The guy's got his heart on his sleeve. He's laying it all out for me. All the things I wouldn't admit I've been wanting to hear from him for years. And I can't manage to say a thing.

"I'm not asking you to forgive me for the past," he says.

"I'm just hoping that you'll give us a chance to build something new."

"Listen." I take a breath. "I'm sorry. For not taking your calls the last few times you reached out, or trusting that this time was different."

"Amos, you don't ever have to apologize to me. You hear me?"

Just then, Flynn comes rushing out. "They found her!"

80

POPPY

I'm in a room filled with lost children. Snow White brought me here after she found me shaking and alone on a bench.

"Are you all right, little one?" she asked in a soft singsongy voice.

"I . . . I can't find my brother and . . . sister," I managed to eke out through my sobs. And as I said the words, I started to cry even harder. And then Snow White wrapped her arms around me, and I wept into her velvety dress. Of course, I know she's not really Snow White, but her hair was dark and her skin was pale, and she had the dress and everything.

She took me to a brightly lit room that looks like it could be in a hospital, except they tried to make it look cheery. The carpet is kind of icky, and there are ragged stuffed animals everywhere. When I got here, I was so upset I was hyperventilating, so they had a nurse check me out. She asked me to try to slow my breathing so she could check my stats, and when they finally got me settled down, she gave me water and animal crackers.

I had to register my name along with the name of the adult in charge. So I gave them Amos's name, and hoped that if Flynn ever found out, she wouldn't be too offended. After all, he is a year older than she is. And he already lives away from home, so he is pretty much an adult.

I realize that I am definitely the oldest lost kid in here, and that just makes me feel even worse. I try not to feel too pathetic as I struggle to stop crying and bring my breath back to normal. The little girl next to me inches closer and closer to me with her blankie in tow, until she's basically in my lap. I wonder how long she's been here . . . waiting. I think about asking her, but before I can, someone calls my name.

81

FLYNN

As we rush to get Poppy, Clay puts his hand on my shoulder and says, "Take a deep breath, sweet girl," and it's only then that I realize I've been holding it.

I've wondered a lot about Amos's father over the years. He's sort of become this mythic figure in my imagination: Clay the artist, the asshole, the ex-husband, the absentee father. And then suddenly here he is. He's smaller than I expected—or maybe it's that Amos got taller while he was away. Clay's strong in his build, but there's something gentle about him.

It's weird—it's like Amos is nothing like him, and yet he's everything like him, too. Like how they both squint when they smile. Somehow, Clay makes Amos make more sense to me. Louisa is all edges, but Amos has a softness to him. A sort of heightened sensitivity I now recognize in his father. Kinda funny that the best parts of Amos could come from a man who's always been so demonized.

As we reach the Baby Center, I try to let myself be calmed by his comforting words. Clay opens the door. I scan the room, and there's Poppy—her cheeks are red, her eyes are teary, and there's a rip in her Ariel sweatshirt. She runs straight into my arms. She's crying and I'm crying, and I'm squeezing her so tight it's like I'm never going to let go.

82

POPPY

I finally stop crying, but I think only because my eyes have run out of tears. I still feel tired and headachy and just not like myself, but Flynn and Amos have their arms around me, and that's helping.

"I was just looking for my camera," I try to explain.

"Poppy, we were terrified. You know you're not supposed to wander off," Flynn says.

"I know. I'm sorry for scaring you. I guess without my medicine—"

"Wait! You haven't been taking your medicine?" Amos interrupts.

Poppy guiltily shakes her head.

"Poppy—are you serious? Why not?" Flynn asks.

"They were in my checked bags," I admit, in a voice so small, because I know I'm in trouble. "I'm sorry. I'm so, so sorry." But instead of yelling at me, Amos and Flynn just look at each other—not like they're mad, just really concerned.

"No, I'm sorry, Pops." Flynn shakes her head. "I should have realized."

"I was hoping that maybe I would be okay without it, but once I started freaking out, I couldn't stop," I tell them. Guess I need those two little white pills more than I thought.

Amos turns to Clay and asks to borrow his phone. He looks up my therapist's number online, then leaves her a message, and Susan calls us back a few minutes later. And just hearing her voice makes me feel better. After we talk for a little bit, Susan asks to speak with Flynn. I hand her the phone, and she steps away for a second.

"Susan called your medicine into a pharmacy nearby," Flynn says when she comes back in. "She said you should be feeling like yourself again in no time. You're going to be fine," she assures me.

"I'm sorry for ruining our last day."

"Are you kidding? All that matters is that you're here, and that you're okay," Amos says as he rubs my back and adds, "And that you never do that again."

"How about we all promise to never run away again?" I suggest.

"I think that's a great idea," Flynn says.

"First stop, pharmacy, then airport," Clay says. I'm glad Amos's dad is here. It's strange seeing the other half of where Amos comes from. I know Mom has a lot of mean things to say about Clay, but so far he seems like a very nice man.

"Thanks," Amos says.

"Anytime, kid. So, are we ready to get outta here?" Clay asks.

"Mind if we take a short detour through Malibu first? We've got a hot Maserati on our hands," Amos says with a wink.

83

AMOS

As I watch my father valiantly guide my sisters through the park and into the sunset, I can't help but think this must be a magical kingdom after all. I mean, we found Poppy. And she's okay. She wasn't maimed or molested or kidnapped or any of the other fifteen thousand horrors I hoped and prayed would not befall her. She made it. Maybe she's more resilient than we give her credit for. Flynn and I, on the other hand, are still reeling—so relieved to be reunited. So, Disneyland, you got me. I'm in. And if that weren't enough magic for one day, who swept in on his white horse (okay, Porsche, but you get the point) to save the day but Clay, of all people. Talk about your least likely knight in shining armor.

"So I was thinking . . ." I turn to Clay. "Maybe I'd come out over spring break? We could hang for a few days?"

"It'd be cool to spend some QT, you and me. Maybe I could finally get you out on the water?"

"I don't know about the surfing part, but I'd like that."

"Wait!" Poppy cries out, and we all stop and turn toward her. "We can't go yet!"

Flynn, Clay, and I look at each other, confused, because for the last however many hours, getting Poppy and getting out of here have been the only things in the world we've wanted to do.

"We can't leave yet," Poppy says again.

"Why not, Pop?" I ask, trying to be patient, but to be honest, I'm pretty exhausted by this point.

"Because," she says sweetly, "we never went on Small World!"

Flynn and I catch each other's eyes. And without another word, we know that Poppy is right. There is just one more thing we have to do. After all, we did make a promise.

FLYNN

I've gotta say, I couldn't wait to get the hell out of the Happiest Place on Earth, but when Poppy pointed out that we never made it back to Small World, what could we do? I mean, at this point, after everything I've put her through, who am I to refuse her anything? So we get in line, and I'm grateful that it's significantly shorter than it was earlier. When it's our turn to board the little boats, Poppy declares that she wants to sit with Clay. I know she's enjoying this rare glimpse of Amos's dad as much as I am. We practically have the ride to ourselves—all the little kids must be at the Christmas show on Main Street, or on their way home, full of tummy aches and fond memories, their sleepy heads gently rattling against their car windows. Poppy and Clay settle in up front, so Amos and I slide into the last row alone.

A warning sounds on a continuous loop. "Please keep your hands and arms inside the ride. Parents, watch your children. Please keep your hands and arms inside the ride." I wave my hand out over the dark, murky waters in mock defiance—it's childish, I know, but I'm too exhausted to be self-aware. Amos grabs my arm. He reaches for my hand, but instead of simply pulling it back inside the safe confines of the boat, he holds it firmly in his. And he doesn't let go. My tired heart stutters, and skips a beat.

"I think our days of living on the edge are done," he warns me, but the thing is, his voice sounds woeful, and I'm not sure he's talking about the ride anymore.

"We had a good run, though," I reply.

"That we did."

"Ready to be back on the right side of the law . . . ?" I say, letting it sound just enough like a question.

"Play it safe—back on the straight and narrow," Amos answers.

"Safe is good," I concede, even though I'm not sure I mean it.

"Safe is boring." Amos sounds about as unconvinced as I am. And then he leans in and kisses me slow and deep. And as much as I know it is not goodbye, a part of me worries that it could be the last kiss of its kind that we share. But with everything happening around us—all the unknowns with our parents—this is how things have to be. For now.

Our boat docks, and that ubiquitous warning comes on again: "Parents, watch your children." And as we emerge out of the darkness back into the bright light, I can't help but be relieved that we made it out the other side—changed, but somehow the same. Amos lets go of my hand, but I tell myself it's okay. I have to believe that if it's meant to be with us, it will happen . . . if the time is right and the stars align.

85

AMOS

Here we are, back at LAX—where it all began. It's hard to imagine that just two days ago we were running so fast, and so hard. We walk slowly, Clay trailing behind us. Across the terminal, I clock Jack and Louisa pacing back and forth in front of the escalators. Even at this distance, I can tell that they are legitimately distraught. Louisa's tightly wound bun is fraying at the sides, and Jack's short-sleeved oxford shirt is sweaty in places and partially untucked. Despite all the reassurances from Clay, their faces remain strained with worry. And I have to admit, seeing them so freaked out makes me feel better. Like it's evidence of their love for us.

They spot us, and relief washes over their faces. As they race toward us, I reach for my sisters' hands, and together we cross the concourse to meet them.

86

FLYNN

"Mommy!" Poppy cries as we approach our parents.

"Poppy! Are you all right?" Louisa bends down and swoops her up into her arms. The whole display is so raw and so surprising that suddenly I find myself in tears as well. My dad wraps his arms around me, and for a moment I'm a little girl, weeping into his shoulder. I'm so absorbed in how good it feels to smell his cologne again, and find comfort in the safety of his strong embrace.

"What the hell were you guys thinking?" My dad pulls away from me and takes me by the shoulders.

"I'm really sorry, Dad. It was my idea to run."

"Flynn, your hair . . . and . . . your nose." He shakes his head, inspecting me. "Please tell me you didn't get a tattoo. How could you do something like this?"

"It was all of us," Amos chimes in from behind me.

Louisa pulls Amos close. She takes his cheeks in her hands

and says, "You scared us, you know that." Then she looks beyond him and spots Clay. It occurs to me that this is probably the first time they've laid eyes on each other in years. We all sort of stand around and watch—like we're waiting for something significant to happen, like lightning to strike or the sky to fall or something. But instead Louisa just says, "How can I thank you?"

And Clay says, "Don't worry about it."

Louisa takes a deep breath and looks at the three of us, tears welling in her eyes. "You did a terrible thing. Do you have any idea what could have happened to you?"

"There are going to be serious consequences when we get home," my dad says.

"It was stupid," I respond. "We know that. But when we heard that you two were getting divorced, and that Dad and I would be leaving—"

"It's just not fair," Poppy interrupts. And my dad and Louisa just stand there, looking at each other, not knowing what to say.

"The thing is," Amos continues, "you guys need to understand that, despite all of your drama, we're a family. And you can't just split us apart."

"Yeah," Poppy chimes in emphatically.

"I'm not moving away, Dad," I announce.

"You're not in a position to negotiate right now, Flynn. I know this is a lot, but it's complicated."

"We'll have plenty of time to sort out all the details once we're back in the city," Louisa offers. But it's not good enough.

Over the loudspeaker, they announce that American flight

739 to JFK is boarding. "That's us. It's the only flight my assistant could get us on. We've got to hurry," Jack says.

"No, Dad," I declare. "We're not getting on that plane until we have your word. New York's my home now."

Jack turns to Louisa. They look at us kids—standing strong, unified, and defiant. Finally, my dad concedes. "I hear you, Flynn. And I promise, we'll find a way to work it out."

"And I want to see Clay more," Amos adds.

Louisa glances over at Clay, surprised, but then nods. "I'm sure we can arrange something."

They call our flight again. "We should really hurry up if we're going to catch this flight," Louisa urges.

Clay puts his hand on Amos's shoulder and gives it a paternal squeeze.

"See you soon, Dad," Amos says. Clay smiles. It's been a long time since Amos called him that.

"Come on, guys. Let's go home," Jack says, rubbing the top of Poppy's head.

"Does this mean we're not in trouble now?" Poppy asks.

"Oh, you're definitely still in trouble," Jack says, putting his arm around her. And with that we say goodbye to Clay, and Los Angeles, and head back home together.

SIX MONTHS LATER

POPPY

I told Annabelle I couldn't have a sleepover since Amos gets in tonight. Annabelle is my new friend. My best friend. Okay, my only friend. But it's just like Amy says to Meg in *Little Women:* "You don't need scores of suitors. You only need one, if he's the right one." Well, I guess that's true for friends, too. Annabelle is kind of a bad girl. Only it turns out she's not really a bad girl at all. She's just misunderstood. Kind of like me. Anyway, once word got out about our whole winter-break adventure, it actually gave me some street cred at school.

One cold January day, out of nowhere, Annabelle came over and sat with me at lunch. And then it happened again the next day. And then it just became this thing that every day we would sit together. My mom is so happy I have a friend that she lets me hang out with Annabelle pretty much whenever I want. And she lives just around the corner from my mom's, which is one of the nice things about her new place. The other nice thing is that it's near Flynn's school, so on Mom's weeks, Flynn comes by to see me on her way back downtown to Dad's. Rosie makes her a snack, and things really don't feel all that different. A few times when Dad went out of town for work, Flynn even slept over. She keeps a toothbrush here and everything. Sometimes I still wake up in the middle of the night not sure where I am, but that's been happening less and less.

AMOS

I don't have to scan the room to find Flynn. She's ensconced in our old corner booth at the Carlyle. Poppy and I cross the bar toward her, not even attempting to hide our smiles.

"Amos picked me up from Annabelle's!" Poppy exclaims as we approach.

"Lucky girl," Flynn says, and we slide in next to her.

And then there's Mac hovering over us, jovial as ever. "Hey, what do you know, the band's back together. What'll it be?"

"The usual," Poppy, Flynn, and I say at the same time.

"One hot fudge sundae, no nuts, extra sauce. Three cherries and three spoons. Coming right up."

I look at my sisters, both so much more grown-up than the last time we were here together. Flynn's kept her hair short, and it looks good like that. I notice the nose piercing is gone, though—it didn't even leave a scar.

"When do you leave for surf camp with Clay?" she asks.

"End of next week."

"So you can come to Flynn's piano recital on Saturday!" Poppy says.

"Recital?" I ask.

"Got a lot of practicing in while I was grounded all winter," she explains.

"Wouldn't miss it." I smile at her.

"Mom's got your room all ready," Poppy says to me. "Guess what color she painted it?" And we all laugh. But still, I know I made the right call to do my senior year back in the city at Collegiate. Boarding school seemed like a solid escape, but I realized (as trite as it sounds) that the person I was running from most was myself. Besides, I hate to admit it, but I was homesick. Granted, it's undoubtedly a new life that I'm returning to, but the most important pieces are the same, even if the geography is a little different.

"Wife, mistress, or daughter?" I ask, gesturing to the couple entering.

The more things change, the more they stay the same. I guess that's the thing about family.

FLYNN

We drop Poppy off at Louisa's, and Amos offers to walk me to Fifth Avenue to catch a cab downtown to my dad's. The summer sun is just beginning to set. Across the park, the windows light up in the iconic buildings of Central Park West: the Beresford and the San Remo.

"You wanna walk for a little?" he asks.

And because it's just light enough outside, and because we can, but mostly because it's me and Amos, I answer, "Yes."

We decide to go through the park. We walk for a while without saying anything. And it feels so good to be back in that comfortable quiet with him. It feels like home. As we cross the park, we find ourselves once again in the Shakespeare Garden.

"What do you say, for old times' sake?" he suggests, gesturing to the Whisper Bench. We take seats at opposite ends, just like that time two years ago. He turns to me and says something softly. But because of the distance and the dimming light, I can't quite read his lips. And then I hear it. Amos's voice in my ear.

"You know I'll always love you—right, Flynn?"

"I love you, too," I say. Because it's the truth. And it always will be.

"It's getting dark. We should get going."

I nod, but we both linger for a moment. We're hesitant to leave—unsure of what the future will bring. If there's one thing we've learned in all of this, it's that life is always changing, and that it's hard to find things, and people, you can hold on to. But once you do, you should never let go. Now that the dust has settled, and our parents' divorce is almost final, I can feel the possibility of Amos and me.

As we walk out of the garden, we pass a plaque with a quote from *Romeo and Juliet.*

"This bud of love, by summer's ripening breath,
May prove a beauteous flower when next we meet."

"You know, it's really good to be home," Amos says. He reaches for my hand, and I take his, our fingers intertwined.

I look at him. "I think it's going to be a really good summer."

ACKNOWLEDGMENTS

This book would not be possible without Allen Fischer—thank you for believing in us from the very beginning. You're the best Coach we could ever ask for. We would also like to thank everyone at Dupree Miller—Dabney Rice, and especially Lacy Lynch. Your tenacity and unwavering support made our dream a reality. Allison Binder, thank you for always being our best advocate.

We are so grateful to Emily Easton for falling in love with Flynn, Amos, and Poppy. Your vision and insight made *Layover* come to life. We couldn't ask for a better home than Random House. To Samantha Gentry, and everyone at Crown, thank you for guiding us through this incredible journey.

To our family and friends—what can we say, thanks for putting up with us (x2). Without your love, this book, and so many other things, would not be possible.

ABOUT THE AUTHORS

Amy Andelson and **Emily Meyer** have been best friends since the seventh grade. As screenwriters, they have worked together on the Step Up franchise, *Naomi & Ely's No Kiss List,* and numerous other TV and film projects. *Layover* is their debut novel. You can follow them on Instagram at @by_amy_and_emily and at byamyandemily.com.